For the adventure in every boy's life this book is dedicated.

In memory of Wisconsin author August Derleth and his young boys mystery series.

Dedicated to my loving wife, and greatest supporter, Mary.

Other books for young readers

by Lon Lawrence

Book 1: THE WOODSTOCK IRREGULARS

Book 2: THE MYSTERY OF THE ABANDONED HOUSE

Book 3: THE MYSTERY OF THE SHINING BROW

SCAN TO SEE AUTHORS BOOKS

© Lon Lawrence

1

I awoke to a flash of lightening. I laid there a while, staring out the window. It was raining heavily and the wind whipped the rain into a frenzy as it lashed against my window pane. The lightening flashed again and I saw it. The shadow of a man walking past the house. I jumped up and ran to the window. I tried to peer into the darkness which was only slightly broken by the yard light across the road at Dean's place. It cast large shadows all across the landscape. Then I saw a the figure of a man dressed in black wearing a snap-brim hat walking along the little creek next to our house heading toward the Pine River, rain pouring off the brim of his hat. He was in and out of the shadows very quickly and I didn't get a good look at him, but why would anyone be out on a night like this? And why would they be cutting between the Walters' store and our house? I stood in the window for almost an hour, unable to go back to sleep, keeping watch. Nothing moved. The figure of the man had disappeared in the shadows.

I don't remember going back to bed, but I remember waking up to the smell of a fresh rain storm and the wrens singing in the trees, and on the ground the robins were pecking for earthworms in the soft, wet earth. The sunlight was dancing on the floor of my room as I swung the window open and the light breeze swayed the curtains creating shadows and sunlight on the floor.

Suddenly I remembered. I remembered the shadow of a man in the night. Had I dreamt it? I might have. I do have scary dreams sometimes. But it seemed so real. With the heavy rain we had, I knew there would be no footprints to show the presence of anyone walking along the creek, and I knew I was the only one that had seen him...if it wasn't a dream, that is.

I could smell bacon frying in the kitchen and hear the sound of wood crackling in the wood stove to heat up breakfast. I knew Ma was getting ready to put a good breakfast on the table. I got dressed quickly into yesterday's dirty jeans, T-shirt and my Red

Ball Jets tennis shoes, which had seen their better days. Summer was almost over and I'd be getting a new pair for school, maybe Keds tennis shoes this time. Wading in water and fishing in the sloughs had pretty much taken their toll on my summer shoes. Canvas shoes don't hold up well to active kids living in the country.

I opened the door and Ma was just serving breakfast, bacon and eggs, chopped fried potatoes and toast and jam, with a large glass of milk. I usually just have cereal for breakfast because I'm always in a hurry and I don't want to wait for a full fried breakfast, but this morning it was already waiting for me.

"Well, it's about time you got up," Ma kidded me. "I thought you might sleep all day."

"Nah, I was really only going to sleep half of the day but I fell out of bed."

"That sounds about right. Now eat your breakfast before you go out to play."

I and my pals, Dean, Arlen and Danny had had a great summer this year. When summer first started we captured some mail thieves from Chicago and that had really started the summer off right. The rest of the summer we spent fishing and swimming and hiking in the woods, rebuilding our fort, which we didn't use any longer because Mr. Tyler had given us permission to use his old garage as our clubhouse, and climbing up on Elephant Foot rock on the hill above Dewey Brown's farm. And we had a lot of rain so the grass grew like crazy and I had to mow lawns every week. But now with fall coming, the grass had slowed down in its growth so I had more time off.

My cousin Cliff had also given Arlen and me our ham radio test and loaned me an old Hallicrafters transceiver that required crystals to be plugged in to change frequency. Arlen's older brother, Ben, had bought Arlen a nice transceiver with a VFO for his birthday so we could send morse code back and forth to each other. We only had a Novice license, which required knowing morse code at five words per minute, so we couldn't talk on the radios, we had to use a telegraph key and send morse code. Our license was only good for one year, then we had to write another test and take a code test at 13 words per minute to get our General license, but that was a longs way off so we hadn't really been studying much for it.

But now summer was coming to an end and school was going to start in a couple weeks, and like all boys, we were dreading going back to school, even though it would be really nice to see some of the kids we hadn't seen all summer.

School wasn't so bad. We all went to a one-room country school about half a mile from Woodstock and there were about 30 students total, counting all eight grades. The grade I was in only had Shelby Planter and myself. Dean and Danny and Arlen were in the grade behind me and there were always a total of five kids in that grade. Besides the three boys there were two girls, Ella Fammerson and Jade Hofferman. Ella had beautiful red hair and Jade was a blonde. I had a crush on Ella.

After breakfast I sauntered over to Dean's place across the road to see if he had anything planned for the day and to tell him about my dream...if it was a dream.

I walked down his driveway to the shop where his dad was standing at the bench working on a lawnmower engine.

"Hi, Mr. Brewster," I hollered above the noise of the air compressor running.

"Well, it's the lost Lone Scout of the Sky," he joshed me, referring to Charles Lindbergh because my birthday on May 21st was on the same day that Lindbergh landed in Paris in 1927. Also my favorite TV show was SkyKing and I really wanted to be a pilot someday.

"Master Brewster is in his office," he nodded toward the door. *Master* was often used in front of the names of underage boys, especially on their mail.

I went into the office, which was the old storefront when this building was a flourishing store in competition to Walters' store across the street.

"Whatcha doing today," I asked.

"I'm putting new fishline on all my reels and my cane pole," he replied. "It's all getting pretty old and breaks too easily."

"Oh, I thought you might be doing something *important*," I kidded him.

"What've you got on your mind today besides your hat?" Dean asked. He was always grouchy in the morning.

"Did you happen to see someone walking down the creek in the middle of the night?" I asked

"Are you crazy? Why would I be up in the middle of the night and why would anyone be outside in that heavy rain we had?"

"I was just asking," I said.

"Ok, spill the beans. You don't ask stupid questions, just cryptic ones. I'm guessing you saw someone last night, right? Tell me what you saw, or thought you saw."

"Well, I *thought* I saw man dressed in black wearing a snap-brim hat walking down the creek by our place during the lightening storm." And I told him the whole story.

"And I thought all the nuts were in the loony bin," he replied.

Unfazed in my story I continued.

"I know it sounds crazy, but if it wasn't a dream, then there is something pretty weird going on. I know there are no footprints after that storm but I though we might retrace his steps from the direction he came and see if anything looks suspicious, just for something to do this morning."

"Ok, I'm finished here, let's go see if we can find any support for your imaginative prowler," Dean replied.

So we left the building and walked the plank across the creek to get on the same side of the creek I had seen the prowler on, then walked toward Pine River which was only about 200 yards away. If the prowler had gone that direction, it was a dead end because you couldn't wade across the Pine River at that area as it was too deep.

We walked to the river and looked around for any clues but of course we didn't find any, so we turned around and walked south, crossing Southshore Lane and heading for Market Street. We saw no telltale evidence along the creek and when we got to Market Street we stopped and looked around. To the west was the large wooden garage where the county road grader was kept. Across the road from that was Harry and Bess Simpson's house. We walked down to the grader garage. The door was open and the grader was gone, indicating Mr. Simpson was out grading roads someplace. There was nothing of interest in the garage. Oils of different kinds for the grader and some old greasy rags to wipe the oil with, a couple of grader tires and a few tools.

We walked out of the garage and went east to the house on the other side of the creek. It was an old abandoned house. It was a majestic old building probably built in the 1920s when Woodstock was a thriving town. The woodwork was heavily adorned with carvings around the doors and window sills. It was in bad repair, having sat for so long without any care, but it was still a stately mansion, three stories high. I would like to have seen it when it was built. It would have been a beautiful building. It was adorned with columns in the front on the stoop, like the old southern mansions, and it had a little picket fence around the property, in bad disrepair. All in all it would have made a great haunted house on Halloween. We walked up to the front door and saw it was cracked open slightly. That would be normal in a larger city, but in this little village there was no crime. Nobody stole anything and if anyone was interested in the old house, they would have locked it back up after looking around, although I assume everyone in Woodstock had seen the inside of it at one time or another. I had lived here for eight years and had never thought about going in it, other than to walk around it and look in the windows. The doors were always locked and had been for many years, but now the front door was open. A little closer look made us think someone had "jimmied" the door as there were marks on the door jamb that indicated a pry bar.

"Looks like we might have had a prowler in the area," I said. "Now maybe you'll believe me when I told you I saw someone."

"You said you *thought* you saw someone. You weren't sure it wasn't a dream, but now it does look like you may have been correct," Dean corrected me.

"Let's go inside and look for clues, since the door is already open and it couldn't be called 'break and entry,'" I suggested.

"No, it could only be called 'illegal entry,'" Dean reminded me. Always cautious and afraid of getting into trouble. Too practical for his own good I always said.

"Well, you stay out here and stand watch. I'll take the risk," I retorted.

"No you don't. You'll probably get in worse trouble if someone isn't watching over your shoulder," said the conscience of the world.

We walked inside. The house was in amazingly good shape yet despite the neglect of many years. All the crown along the tops of the walls in each room were carefully hand carved as were the wainscoting along the bottom of each wall. The wainscoting, which consists of baseboard molding, wall panels, and a chair rail or top molding, looked like many paneled doors along the wall.

The hand railing on the stairwell was also hand carved and had an unusual twist to it as it ascended the stairs. There were still old chandeliers hanging from the ceilings that looked rather expensive, and I was surprised they had been left behind. I wondered why anyone would just abandon a house like this. Surely it would have been worth a lot of money at one time.

We looked at the floor by the door sill and there were footprints, muddy footprints by the door, from the night before. It was pretty obvious the prowler I saw had been in this house, but for what reason?

We looked around but didn't find anymore footprints. Somebody had carefully wiped them or swept them and only missed the ones by the front door. They were trying to cover up what they did and where they went in this house, and you don't need an active imagination to know that was very suspicious. We carefully searched the empty house for clues but could find none. There was very little evidence to go on. The back door was still locked and all the windows were closed and locked. With no furniture in the house there was very little to look at. It was just an empty house with a secret that it wasn't giving up.

We pulled the door closed on the way out but the door jamb

was broken where the break-in occurred so there was no way to secure it.

"What do you make of that," I asked.

"There's definitely been a prowler in here, I can't deny that with the evidence, and it probably was the guy you saw in the rain, but we certainly don't have any idea who it was nor what they wanted. I don't think it looks like much of a case at this point," Dean replied. "We don't even have enough evidence to start looking for more answers."

I had to agree. It looked like a dead-end, unless there would be a reason for him to come back, in which case we'd have to keep an eye on the place for several days just in case we could gather another sighting and more evidence.

It was getting near dinner time when we finished so we both headed home to wait for dinner and give this some more thought.

I couldn't get it out of my head, the picture of that scary man dressed in black with a large snap-brim hat, in a heavy rain, walking along the creek, not in a hurry. It was like an apparition. He looked like Lamont Cranston, otherwise known as *The Shadow.* I wasn't going to sleep very well for a while!

2

The next day I called Arlen on his ham radio on 30 meters, the only band dedicated to morse code. After calling a few times I got his reply. In morse code I called "WN9OLD DE (this is) WN9JFZ" three times and wait. If he had his radio on, he would answer the call.

He came back to me and we talked back and forth for a while to hone our morse code skills. I told him I was planning on coming up after dinner to talk over something with him. He said he'd be home, so we signed off.

I was also building a little pocket transceiver with transistors, which were available for hobbyists in 1957 and there were lots of plans in Boy's Life Magazine, ARRL magazine (American Radio Relay League) and in Popular Science magazine. They were very simple to build but only had 100 milliwatt power, unlike our big tube radios that had 5 watts. However, I was looking for something to carry in emergencies that might come in handy, and I was just waiting on one more transistor from Radio Shack so that I could finish the project. I was pretty good at building electronics stuff because I had built a Knight Kit Star Roamer 5-band shortwave radio. That took several weeks and was a lot of fun.

After dinner I rode up to Arlen's and we played with his new ham radio and I showed him the plans for a pocket transceiver which he was very interested in and said he might send for the parts and built one, too, if mine worked.

We called CQ, dah-di-dah-dit dah-dah-di-dah, on his radio for a while, which is the call for "calling anyone." But we didn't get any answers as the signals don't reach very far during the daytime.

Then we took his dog King for a walk in the woods. The hickory nuts were starting to fall so we took a sack along to pick up some for his mom for baking.

When we got up on the hill we sat down for a while to talk. I told him about my encounter with the prowler.

"I haven't seen him for two nights now that I've been watching, but I can't stay up all night, so he could have easily gotten by me."

"That is a real mystery as to what he was up to," Arlen agreed. "It's pretty obvious he's up to no good or he wouldn't have to be sneaking around like that. But if he doesn't come back, we'll never know what it was all about."

"We searched the house pretty well, but it wasn't hard to do because the house is empty. There were no clues as to why he was there, but it was important enough that he thought he needed to sweep his footprints away," I said.

"Where do you go from here?" Arlen asked.

"Just watch and wait," I answered. "There's nothing else I can do yet. But for now let's pick up some hickory nuts for your mom."

We picked up about half a paper grocery sack of hickory nuts so that should result in some great deserts like brownies, chocolate date cake, cookies and more.

"I talked to Ruth   LeBohne the other day when I saw her at the store," I said. "She always hires a kid to help her on the little farm each summer and I need money to buy a new bike because Ma made me put the reward money from our last caper into my college fund. Ruth said she hadn't picked out anyone for next summer yet but if I wanted the job, she'd put my name at the top of the list and contact me next summer. It's only for about 2 months so I'll still have a full month off before school starts," I told Arlen.

"That's great if that's what you really want to do. Farm work can be hard work."

"It's not a big farm. She only has one milk cow, but she needs the lawn mowed and fences repaired and work like that. I hear she pays you after each job you do. When you finish digging a fence post hole, she hands you a dime. Mow that big lawn and she hands you a dollar, things like that. You go home with a pocketful of change each day. I hope it adds up to a lot of money."

"Well, you'll have to give up being a detective for a couple months," Arlen kidded.

And that was true. Work always interfered with having fun in life.

Mrs. Bailey asked me to stay for supper and she didn't have to ask twice. Mr. Bailey came in from milking and we had a baked potato, roasted chicken and light gravy for the potato, and corn on the cob. For desert she had pumpkin pie, and the pumpkin was from her own garden.

I went home about six in the evening and rode around Woodstock a little, still mulling over the prowler I'd seen. I decided to stop over at Grandpa's and see what he thought about the whole situation.

"Hi old-timer," Grandpa said as soon as I stepped into the house.

"Hi Grandpa, you doin' anything special?" I asked

"Just reading a good book about the opening of the west by Irving Stone called 'Men to Match My Mountains'," he said. "You should read it. I think it's the best story about opening the west that I've ever read."

"I'll have to read that when you're done," I said. "Say, Grandpa, there was a prowler the other night."

"A prowler?" Grandpa asked. "What makes you think there are any prowlers in Woodstock?"

So I told him the complete story including our investigation of the house.

"That's interesting enough to bring in the Woodstock Irregulars, I'd say," Grandpa loved picking on me about our detective agency. "How do you plan on catching this bad guy?"

"Well, we don't know what to do next. If he only comes around in the middle of the night, there's a good chance we'll never know it because I can't stay up all night watching for him."

"I'd set some traps for him," Grandpa suggested. "For instance, you could put a thread across the entrance to the house and when it's broken, you'll know he's been there. Replace the thread and keep an eye on it. You might find a pattern so you'll know when to watch the house. Of course a good detective would do a stakeout, like sleep in the house, but I don't think your Ma would go along with that."

"That thread is a great idea, Grandpa, and we could put some across other rooms in the house so we'll know what part of the house he's going to! I'll go get Dean and start working on that this evening before dark."

"Well, just don't get in any trouble. You probably shouldn't be in the house because that could be trespassing, but that house has been empty for so many years that I doubt anyone would really care. In fact, I doubt anyone in the neighborhood even knows who it belongs to. But don't tell your Ma too much until you have some evidence. You know how she is."

"Boy, do I!" I said.

I went over Dean's and pitched our plan to him. He wasn't even afraid of getting into trouble, yet, and was willing to help. He said he had a lot of thread in the office that he used to tie flies for fishing, so he grabbed a spool of that and a roll of scotch tape and we headed up to the house.

When we got to the house, we went inside and started looking for the best and most obscure spots to place the thread. Of course we placed one across the stairway and across the doorways into each room. And as we were standing in the kitchen, looking around, I glanced out the window and there was a strange black and white car turning off Woodstock drive onto Market Street. I paused for a minute to watch it. Dean saw me and came to the window, but instinct told me to move away from the window and watch in hiding.

"Look, a strange car in town," I said.

"It certainly doesn't belong to anyone that lives in or near Woodstock," Dean replied.

"Keep low, so he can't see us," I said.

It was a 1957 Rambler four-door. White on the top and black on the bottom. It was driving very slowly and the driver was staring at the house. He was dressed in black and wearing a large snap-brim hat. It *had* to be *him*. The only problem is, we couldn't go outside to get a license number. He drove on by and turned left onto Wolf Lane and was soon out of sight.

"Well, if that don't beat all," I said. "I'm sure that's the guy I saw the other night and now he's driving around the area and casing the joint. I wonder why?"

"You're sure that was him?" Dean asked.

"Positive. Too many coincidences, and as we say in the detective business, 'there are no such things as coincidences.' He was dressed just like the guy I saw and he's obviously casing the joint."

"Don't let your imagination over-power your logic. We often get strange cars driving through town. Well, maybe not often, but we do see one from time to time. He might be looking for a place to buy and he saw this empty house."

Dean was getting cautious on me again.

"First of all, when's the last time we've had anyone new buy a place in Woodstock? Right. Never in our lifetime. This place is stuck in time. Nobody moves away, nobody sells, nobody dies, and nobody comes into the area unless they are renting and working one of the local farms. And they are never here more than a year. But the houses in Woodstock itself never change hands," I replied. "No, that was him alright and I've got an idea. Let's go outside and look at the tire prints, then let's try to follow them backward and see where they came from."

"That's the best idea you've had all day," Dean said. So we finished up in the house and set a string across the front door and left. We went to the gravel road and saw the fresh tracks.

"We'd better do this right. Let's go get our bikes and follow them or we'll be walking all day," I said.

So we ran back down the creek and got our bikes then went back up to the house and started carefully following the tracks back down Market Street and onto Woodstock Drive. Then it crossed Southshore Drive and kept going north. We followed it to Kingsman's place and gave up.

"Ok, we know it's going to go down to County D and since that's a blacktop road, we can't follow the tracks, so let's go back to our starting point and see how far it goes down Wolf Lane," I told Dean.

We turned around and went back to the house then picked up

the track again and turned down Wolf Lane. We followed it all the way to County D again, at the first entrance to Woodstock, and saw the tracks turned to the right, toward Richland Center.

"Well, that's that," I said. "We are pretty sure he comes from the direction of Richland Center, but no way to find out where. Looks like we've hit a dead end again."

"Aww, most of your hare-brained schemes are dead-ends," Dean complained. "It's getting late so let's go home and get up early to go fishing in the morning and we can check on the house every day to see when he's been back."

That sounded like a good idea so we headed home.

The next morning, bright and early, I got dressed and made an egg salad sandwich from some sliced boiled eggs and mayonnaise Ma had in the refrigerator. I grabbed a bottle of pop and an apple and put it all in a paper lunch sack, like we carried our lunches in during the school year, then I got my fishing pole and some tackle and went to Dean's place.

Dean was in his office, as usual, and he was in an unusually cheery mood.

"What's up, smiley," I joshed him.

"I was just thinking about earlier this summer when you got us into all that trouble with the law and we ended up in jail, not once, but twice."

"I would think that would make you pretty glum," I said candidly. "You were the only one that actually got upset about the whole case we solved."

"Yes, I was, but when I look back on it, it could have been a lot worse. I'm smiling because I'm happy that we didn't go to Juvenile Hall until we turned 18 and could then be sent to prison. It was quite an experience, but I sure don't want any more like that. Let's just hope I don't fall for anymore of your wild schemes that always seem to turn sour," he said.

"Well, I hate to spoil such a good mood, but you forgot that you made $250 reward money from helping solve that case and now you are already into it again by breaking into that old house with me."

"I'll admit, that money made it all worthwhile in the end, and furthermore, we didn't break into that house yesterday. The door was open on an old abandoned house. The word 'abandoned' implies that no one knows who it belongs to so that makes it sort of 'community property.' And besides, all we did was look around and left it exactly like we found it. What court could convict us of anything on that very poor case?" Dean confessed. He was reaching at straws to justify the fact that he was enjoying himself, whether he wanted to admit it or not.

"OK." I didn't want to disagree and ruin his happy spirit. "Where do you want to fish today?"

"I was wondering if there might be some fish west of here at the big swimming hole at the bend in the river," he suggested.

"I don't think anyone has been swimming there all summer," I said. It was too deep for us, so we very seldom ventured into those waters. "The fish might have found that to be a very peaceful water hole."

So we headed up the Pine River to the big swimming hole. It was late summer and the air was still with a bright blue sky and the roosters were crowing up on the hill at the Drayson farm. They made noise from morning until night.

As we got closer to the big swimming hole the land got wooded on the south side of the river, and we could see grey squirrels and an occasional red fox squirrel scampering from tree to tree, picking up their winter storage of hickory nuts. The red fox squirrel was chattering away warning everyone to stay away from his cache of nuts.

A blue jay was sitting at the top of a large maple tree giving his loud jeer, and then some clear whistled notes and some gurgling sounds. Probably scolding the squirrels. The air was starting to smell of fall coming. Pretty soon the leaves would turn color and start falling off the trees, then the woods would have that musty smell of old dried leaves. I loved to breathe in the odors of the woods in the fall.

Next month squirrel season would open and Dad and I would bring home some squirrels for the meat and Ma made great brown gravy from them. I loved squirrel gravy.

I came from a family of hunters. Dean nor Arlen did, although Danny was a great hunter also. My dad harvested partridge and pheasants when they were in season, and he always brought home a deer for fresh venison during the deer season. I was still too young for most of that, but I was honing my hunting skills on the plentiful supply of squirrels in the fall.

We fished all morning and caught two bullhead, lots of suckers, which we released, and a few of the large minnows. We didn't get much fish for eating but we had a good morning fishing. We broke for dinner and dived into our lunch sacks. Dean had brought a peanut butter and jelly sandwich along with a banana, some grapes, which he shared with me, and he had two bags of potato chips, which he also shared.

After dinner we decided to pursue our case and go check on the thread at the house, so we headed back home with our catch. We might even have bullhead to eat for supper.

3

We got to the house about one o'clock on our bikes. I checked the string on the front door and it had been broken so we knew we were in luck.

"Hey, look at this," Dean observed. "The mystery man broke our string."

"Or someone else has been in the house," I countered.

"Why throw water on the fire?" Dean asked.

"Let's go in and look around and see where all he went," I suggested.

We walked to each doorway and examined the thread. One was broken going into the study, but that was the only one.

"Well, if someone else was in here looking around, they didn't go very far, just into one room. I'd say that rules out a second person being here. Our mystery man had a reason to go into this room and only this room," I proclaimed.

"Sounds logical," Dean replied. "But the big question now is *why*."

"I'd sure like to be here while he's in this room," I said. "If we could watch what he does, we might have a clue what he's looking for. We've looked all over this room and I don't see anything out of the ordinary."

"Let's look for new tire prints out in the road, "Dean suggested.

We walked out to the road and looked for tire prints. They were easy to spot because his tires had a distinct pattern that I remembered from the other day. There they were, big and bold. He had cruised up and down the road in front of the house several times to make sure there was no one around. He had parked the car in the driveway of the house and turned around and headed back out the same way he went last time. We followed the prints as far as the blacktop road and they turned toward Richland Center again.

"Well, that settles that," Dean said. "Same problem as before.

THE MYSTERY OF THE ABANDONED HOUSE

We have no idea where he's going."

"We need a new plan," I said. "What do you say to a couple nights of camping out?"

"Sure, I like camping. Where do you want to go?"

"Let's camp on the balcony of the upstairs of that old house. That way we can watch it all night. If anyone comes, it'll wake us up and we can see what they are doing. With no street lights in town it will be nice and dark and he'll never see us unless he shines the flashlight up on the balcony on his way to the house, and I seriously doubt he'd have any reason to do that unless we make some noise," I replied.

"Oh No! You're not getting me into that sort of thing. What if he has a gun? And if he sees us, he might start shooting! It's way too dangerous. Watching someone from a distance is one thing, but being that close to someone who's already a suspicious person could be very dangerous. Let's just pretend that whatever he is doing is none of our business...like it really is!" Dean replied with a yellow streak a mile wide.

"OK, you stay home and I'll get Arlen to go with me."

"Go ahead. You two egg-heads can both get shot. I'll visit your grave and put flowers on it."

"Ok, have it your way. I'll tell Arlen you are a big yellow chicken and I need someone dependable to back me up."

"Tell him anything you want to. I don't need any more trouble than you got me into earlier this summer."

I didn't say any more. I knew he was going to have a real fight with his conscience and his natural curiosity. It was always a big fight between having an adventure and staying safe. If he has enough time to think about it, adventure usually wins out. We went back home and Dean went to his office to brood. I went over to Grandpa's place.

"Hi Grandpa," I hollered as I walked up his sidewalk. He was sitting on the porch reading the paper.

"It's about time you report in and tell me how your case is going," he said.

"Well, it's kind of a stalemate right now. We put the thread across the doorway and each room. Today we went back and the doorway thread was broken and the thread into the study, but we couldn't find any clues as to why he was in there. He hadn't been in any other room. Besides that, while we were in the house the other day putting the thread on the entrances, a 1957 black and white Rambler drove by going really slow and watching the house. He didn't see us, but we were watching him from a window. I swear it was the same guy that I saw in the rain the other night. We followed his car tracks again today, same as yesterday when he drove by, and they went back to the blacktop on County D and headed toward Richland Center, the same as last time. Right now I'm trying to get Dean to go on a camping trip with me."

"A camping trip might be fun. Maybe as you relax in the wild and ponder on the problem you'll come up with some answers," said Grandpa.

"That's not the kind of camping trip I had in mind," I said. "I want to camp on the balcony of the old house and keep an eye on it for a couple of nights. Dean is being too cautious, as always, and wants to sit this one out, but I think he'll come around before long."

"Well, that might get a little dangerous. What if that guy is armed?"

"I thought of that, but we'll be up real high on the second floor and it's a new moon, so it will be really dark. There would be no reason for him to shine a light up on the second floor of the house. I think it would be pretty safe and we might be able to learn more."

"Well, I wouldn't tell your Ma what you're planning on doing. Just leave it at, 'we are going camping.' If she pins you down you'll have to use your own judgement about fibbing to your Ma. I'd just tell her that you haven't decided yet, wherever you feel like pitching a tent and hope she buys that."

"That sound like a good plan," I said.

"It's easier to ask for forgiveness than ask for permission." Grandpa laughed.

"I've got to find out what is so interesting in that house that we can't find."

I said goodbye and left to go home and adjust the chain on my bike. It was getting close to suppertime so I decided to find things to do around the house while I waited for supper. I'd go see Dean again after supper and try to shame him into going with me.

After supper the whippoorwills were starting their evening call and the dew was starting to form on the blades of grass, getting my tennis shoes wet while crossing the yard. I made my way to Dean's to work on his curiosity.

"Hey, let's go for a ride before dark," I said.

"Ok, let's ride up by Dewey's place. I want to see if I can see anyone up on the hill by Elephant Foot rock. I saw smoke up that direction this evening," Dean suggested.

Dean was still on the case, even if he didn't want to admit it. He was hooked. We hopped on our bikes and rode up Woodstock drive south towards Dewey's place, about half a mile up the road. About halfway to Dewey's place we looked up at the big rocks and there definitely was a small trail of smoke up there, about the size of a small campfire.

"I wonder who could be camping up there," Dean asked.

"It's obvious it isn't us and we are the only kids around here that would go camping up there. This warrants an investigation, but coming up from the face of this hill would put us out in the open and be easily seen approaching. It might be totally non-threatening, but then again, we should play it safe. Let's go back down to Southshore Drive and ride up the hill and go up Main Street past Drayson's place, and past old George's place at the end and follow the cow trail up and around from the blind side of the rocks, just to be safe," I suggested.

"That sounds like the best ideal," Dean agreed.

So we rode back down the road to Southshore, turned left, went up the hill and turned left on Main Street. When we went well past George's place there was that Rambler we were watching for, parked in the path. I wrote down the license number on a pad of paper I had in my pocket. We left our bikes in the grass and proceeded on foot. It was a steep climb but soon we were at the base of the rock on the backside.

I said, "Let's take this easy path up to the top of the rock. It's flat up there and we can crawl on our bellies across the rock to the other side and look down and see what our prowler is doing with a fire up here." Dean was in agreement.

We climbed the rock on a well-worn path and when we got to the top, we dropped to our bellies and crawled across to the other side. As we got close to the edge we were very careful to keep our heads down and we crawled to the edge where we could see down to the bottom. There was that same man, the prowler we had been looking for, cooking a meal over a campfire. He had a small pup tent with a bedroll in it. He was planning on spending some time here and it was a perfect place to keep an eye on the old house.

We quickly crawled back the way we came, back down the rock, and didn't say a word until we got back to our bikes.

"Well, if that don't beat all. That's one mystery solved. We thought that guy was living in Rockbridge or Richland Center but it appears he has moved his operation closer so he can keep an eye on the house. I'd sure like to know what he's up to," I said.

"It's pretty obvious that there's something hidden in that house that he's been looking for, I'd say," Dean concluded.

"Yes, that, *and* the fact that he feels he has to watch the place constantly means he's either onto us hanging around the place, or he's worried about someone else who might also be casing the place," I said. "I guess we'd better cancel that camping trip on the balcony for now because he's watching the place too closely... but...we can camp in our fort which is directly in line with the house and we can keep an eye on it, too!"

That sounded like a good idea to Dean and I didn't have to keep working on his curiosity and shaming him to get him to go camping because we camp quite often at the fort.

We raced back down the hill to make it home before dark and made quick plans to camp out at the fort the next night or two.

The first thing I did was call Danny and gave him the license number from the 1957 Rambler. His brother was a cop in Mazomanie and had helped us out with a license number when we were on the case of the mail thieves earlier this summer, so I told Danny what we were up to and asked him to see if his brother would help us.

"Well, I don't know," said Danny. "I don't want to make up another story, and he knows how we solved that last case with his help, it was in all the papers. I think he'd be willing to help us if I told him the truth."

"I'll leave that up to you. Just let me know if he's willing to help. If not, I know a cop in Richland Center who's a friend of my dad's who might help. But I hate to ask him and bring a stranger into our confidence."

"Ok," Danny replied. I'll let you know, probably by tomorrow. You call me." I agreed to that.

After letting our folks know we were going camping for a couple nights up at the fort, everything was set. We spent the next morning getting our supplies carried up to the fort. We loaded everything in a Radio Flyer wagon and went up the driveway to the old Tyler house and cut across the field to the fort where we set up camp. We figured we would be less likely to be seen going to the fort if we didn't use the road to get there. We brought along a Coleman stove to heat our food so we wouldn't make any smoke with a campfire.

We sat around the fort all afternoon, snacking on some chips and drinking Dr. Pepper, and reading. We had brought along plenty to keep us busy reading. Comic books, Popular Mechanics, and Popular Science magazines were our favorite reading materials, but we kept an eye on the house all the time also. Nothing happened all day so we turned in early at sundown so that we wouldn't show any lights to alert anyone, but we took turns watching the place during the night as much as we could.

About midnight a car drove up the road almost to the fort with the headlights off and turned right, then drove down Market Street and stopped in front of the house. I saw the dome light come on as they opened the car doors and exited, two men, but I couldn't see them very well from the dome light in the car. They had really small penlights to show their path as they walked toward the house and went inside. I woke Dean.

"What do you think they're doing?" Dean asked.

"I don't know yet," I replied. They just got here and it's for certain we can't see what they are doing inside."

We could see the light of the two penlights moving around in the house and it looked like a good time to get closer to do a little sleuthing work. We couldn't see our hand in front of our faces as it was a new moon and black as the ace of spades, but we each had penlights also, which, if used carefully, wouldn't give our position away. We left the fort and walked quietly down the road to the house, then turned into Wilbur Braithwaite's yard and sneaked around back of the old house. We were just working our way up alongside the old house when we heard a noise that made us pause. The sound of another car approaching without headlights. It stopped in front of the first car that had arrived and I could see by the dome light when the driver's door opened that it was the original prowler from up on Elephant Foot rock. We stood very still as he entered the house and walked back toward the study.

We watched through the window as the prowler quietly, and with gun drawn, walked into the study.

4

The first two guys were down on the floor on their knees, apparently looking for something. They didn't hear the third guy enter the room.

"Can I help you boys find something?" The prowler asked.

Startled, the two men jumped to their feet and immediately reached for their guns, but thought better of it, seeing they were already covered.

"Why, Larry. It's a coincidence finding you here," the taller man said.

"Not nearly as coincidental as finding you here, Sweeny," Larry said. So now we had a name for the prowler, Larry something, and one of the new guys...Sweeny.

"Just what exactly are you looking for?" Larry asked.

"Oh, come on, Larry, you know darn well what we are looking for. You ran out on us. We thought you were trying to cheat us out of our fair share," Sweeny replied. "You don't have any need for that gun, Let's just talk this over."

"Talking time is done," Larry replied. "I should just shoot you and leave the bodies here for the neighbors to find and call the sheriff. When they are done investigating, I can go back to my work. But that might take too long. They'd have this murder scene locked up tight for a long time, and I don't have that much time."

"Let's make a deal, then," offered Sweeny.

"I tried making a deal with you before, but you double-crossed me," Larry said. "I can't trust you anymore."

"You can't keep the treasure all to yourself," Sweeny said. "We are entitled to some of it too. After all, it was my idea and my plans that pulled-off this job. We heard through the grapevine that you had told old Joe Hanson, who was getting paroled when you went in the slammer, where you had left the treasure and asked him to hide it in some old house you owned in Woodstock, but he died before he could tell you where he hid it. Isn't that how the story goes, Larry?"

"You think you're so smart. You lost all rights to any claims you had when you tried to double-cross me," Larry replied. "You left me holding the bag. I've paid for this treasure with 20 years of my life. You two should clear out, and if I see you anywhere in this area again, the sheriff is going to have two unexplained bodies on his hands. Now get in your car and vamoose. And don't let me catch you around here again."

"Ok, Ok, Don't get sore. I can see you haven't found it yet anyway, so we can just bide our time. You can do the work for us, how's that sound to you?" Sweeny sneered.

"It sounds like you are planning something bigger than you can handle," Larry said. "I suggest you forget about this caper and go find something else to do if you want to live. Now scram."

With that Sweeny and the other man quickly left the house and drove away. Larry stayed behind awhile to look around to try to see if they had discovered anything. Feeling secure that they hadn't, Larry also turned and left. We were still standing under the window of the study.

"Well that clears up a lot, except we still don't know what they are looking for," Dean said.

"Well that turn of events is bound to change Larry's plans. Whatever he's looking for, he obviously had an idea that someone else would be coming to look for it too, and now that the cat is out of the bag, he's going to have to step up his time-table to get to it before the other two guys find it. Now it will be a game of cat and mouse to see who finds it first without getting shot," I replied. "The bad part is, now all three of the gangsters will be keeping an eye on the place and it will be difficult for us to do any searching."

We went back to the fort and spent the rest of the night trying to sleep. A great horned owl was calling 'who? who?' in the tree over our heads. He was wondering 'who' and we were wondering 'what.' It was quite a mystery as to what kind of treasure was hidden. The clues we had so far didn't really give us many answers. All we really knew was that three men were all looking for some sort of treasure. We knew nothing about the history of that old house so it looked like it was time for a trip to the public library in Richland Center to use the microfiche to look back through old newspapers to see if there was any missing treasures in the area. It was only Wednesday, so we'd have to wait until Saturday and bum a ride with Dad to town and do some research while Dad worked until noon each Saturday at the garage. We had pretty much reached a dead end for now. Maybe it was time to bring in the other Woodstock Irregulars and discuss the problems and see if anyone could come up with a good idea.

I finally fell asleep and didn't wake until the meadowlarks started singing in the morning.

It was now about 6:30AM and the sun was breaking between the leaves of the trees where we were sleeping and it was shining in my eyes. I rolled over to get out of it and noticed Dean was also awake.

"How'd you sleep," I asked.

"Terrible," he said. "I kept dreaming about getting caught by those guys and being shut in a small, dark room, and we couldn't get out. We were running out of air and I'd wake up gasping for breath. What an awful night."

"You were still remembering when we got caught in John Walters' farmhouse by those mail thieves on our first case and they locked us in the cellar," I said. "That memory played right into our current predicament. We won't get caught like that again." I hoped. "Let's fry up some eggs and toast and then pack up. I don't think we need to watch that place for a while. Those three guys will be so busy watching each other that no one will dare to go near the house. Besides, we've got other business to attend to now."

"What kind of business are you talking about?" Dean asked.

"I think we need to assemble the whole team and kick around the problem, sort of brainstorming, and see if anyone can come up with some ideas for our next move. I also need to find out if Danny got the license number for us. We've got a lot to do before

Saturday."

"What are we going to do Saturday?"

"We are going to hitch a ride with Dad to the public library and do some historical research about the history of this area and this old house. I'd like to find out if there's any records of a lost treasure."

"Ok," Dean replied. "That certainly sounds like something that's a lot more safe than what we almost blundered into last night."

"Well, at least that's the second mystery solved. We got their names and we have some idea what they are looking for now," I proclaimed.

"That's true except we don't know what the treasure is. It could be money, or important papers, or artifacts, just about anything. That makes it more difficult for us if we don't know what we're looking for."

That was a fact. We didn't know what we were looking for. Hopefully the library would give us a clue.

When we got home we split up and Dean went to call Danny and I went home to call Arlen. Ma was in the kitchen baking something and didn't pay much attention to me except to ask how the camping trip went.

"That was a short camping trip. Did you run out of food?" She asked.

"No, Ma, we just wanted to do some fishing and maybe do some bike riding," which was the truth because we'd have to ride our bikes to meet the other guys. I didn't want Ma listening in our my phone conversation so I went to my bedroom and turned on my shortwave transceiver and gave Arlen a call in morse code. "WN9OLD DE WN9JFZ." After about five calls he came on the air and we had a very short conversation. I told him we had a new case and needed his and Danny's help and told him to meet us at the old fort. He replied and we signed off.

I went over to see Dean and he had invited Danny to meet us at the fort also and he said that Danny had some license information for us. Half an hour later we were all gathered at the fort.

"Danny, what did you find out on the license number?" I asked.

"My brother said it belongs to a Larry Thompson who's address is listed at 310 West Elm, in Milwaukee. I don't know if that helps us much. We don't know anyone in Milwaukee that can check it out."

"Well, at least the name checks out," I said. Now we have a last name to go with the first name we got last night, so we can add that to our research at the Library on Saturday."

I filled in Arlen and Danny the full story of how this case started and what we had learned so far.

"This sounds like a pretty dangerous case," Arlen said. And he's not usually scared of anything. "Three guys that are after each other with guns. I wouldn't want to get caught in the crossfire."

"You're starting to sound like Dean," I said.

"Aww leave me alone," said Dean. "I just like to weigh all the information before jumping in and doing something stupid that might land us in jail or worse, get us shot!" He was always afraid of going to jail.

Arlen replied, "I was just making an observation. This looks like a pretty complicated case at this point. Too little information and too many danger points. We need to go slow and be very careful."

"Have you asked John Walters if he knows anything about that house," Danny asked.

"No, but that's a good idea," I said. "Let's go down to the store in a few minutes and Arlen, you put on your really dumb and innocent look and pump John for information. Right now let's examine what we have and see if anyone has a good idea for our next step."

"How about more stakeouts and watch them some more?" Arlen asked.

"We thought that might be a waste of time since they are busy watching each other to see who goes to the house next, so none of them will be anxious to make any moves. We might watch that house for a week or more before anything happens, and we might miss it anyway because we can't watch it 24 hours a day for more than a couple days if all four of us are taking turns," I said.

"You're probably right on that," Danny agreed. "But what about the four of us exploring the house?"

"I think that would be too dangerous. With them watching the house, we don't want them watching us, too," I said. "Right now we're not sure they even know we are interested in it and I'd like to keep it that way. If we go in at night, we'd need flashlights and if they are watching the house it would give us away. During the daytime might work if we go in a window where they can't see us, but let's put that idea on our list of things to try and see if we can come up with a better idea before we try that. We don't want to get caught in the house."

All agreed that was probably the best idea for now, but secondary to going to town and doing some research. Search the papers for news about a Larry Thompson, and for news about a lost treasure. It would also be worth our while to find out who owns the house and then do a search for any news about that house. We might get lucky and one of those searches could give us enough clues to draw some more conclusions. So we agreed to hold off on going into the house until Dean and I get back from town and doings some research.

"Why don't we all go to town," Danny asked. "You've got a lot of work to do and not many hours to get it done. If all four of us were working on it, we could accomplish a lot."

That sounded like a better idea, so we decided to let Dad know all four of us wanted to spend half a day in town. That would be easy to pull off. So we all agreed on the new plan and then headed down to the store.

"Hiya John," I said as we walked into the store. John was sitting behind the counter reading the Madison State Journal newspaper as usual and the store was empty, also as usual. "I see you are swamped with customers today. How do you wait on all of them?" I teased him.

"Well, hello boys. It's good to see some familiar faces. Let's see if I can find the time to wait on four more customers. I'm pretty busy with all these other folks," he said with a big grin on his face.

Arlen stepped up to the counter, looking like he just fell off the turnip truck, looking at the shelves of candy bars.

"I'd like a candy bar," he said. We just stood back and watched the situation comedy unfold.

"Which one do you want?" John asked. The trap was set and the bait was taken.

"Gosh, I don't know. They all look so good. I'd like something that would give me some energy and maybe make me a little smarter," Arlen said.

"Well, that's a pretty big order," said John. "Any of them will give you energy but I don't know which one would make you smarter. Why do you want to be any smarter? Do you need help figuring something?"

"Oh, well, I'm pretty hungry. I read someplace that if you get hungry your brain slows down. Give me one of those Butterfinger bars, please. You see, we've been trying to figure out how long that old abandoned house on Market Street has been empty and maybe who owns it. But we haven't found anyone who knows anything about the place."

John was hooked. He liked to talk about the history of Woodstock.

The rest of us had walked over to the pop cooler and were trying to look like we were disinterested in what they were talking about as we sorted through and discussed the different flavors of pop while trying to overhear everything they said.

"Well, I'll tell ya," John said. "That house has been empty a lot longer than you boys have been alive, I can tell ya that. I don't remember the exact year, but sometime about 1850, some old guy by the name of Hillsboro moved into the area. He started a town up north of here which bears his name, Hillsboro. I heard he had come from a pretty rich family somewhere over by Milwaukee, although I have no idea what they made their money from. He left Hillsboro in about 1855 and moved down here and bought some land and was very instrumental in the building of Woodstock, which was originally called Siresville, and he helped finance the building of your school house, which was built in 1884. You probably noticed the big stone in the peak of the schoolhouse with the date on it. But one day he packed up everything and moved back to Hillsboro. Hillsboro has done very well, much better than Woodstock. At one time Woodstock had several mills, a blacksmith shop and a brick factory. But Woodstock never really took off and populated like Hillsboro did. It's about 20 or 30 times bigger than Woodstock, but about one-fourth the size of Richland Center. So the town carries his name and he never came back to Woodstock and for some reason the house never sold. It's just sat empty."

"Was there any mystery, or anything exciting about that old empty house?" Arlen asked with a real dumb look on his face.

"Oh, I don't know that there was anything much of a mystery about it," John said. "Like all empty houses it's been accused of being haunted. People have claimed to see lights moving around in the house, let's see, that was after I opened the story, maybe in the 1940s, but there hasn't been any talk about hauntings for many years now."

"Oh, that's sure exciting information," Arlen nodded. "I do like a good story."

"Are you Woodstock Irregulars professional ghost hunters now?" John kidded us.

"Oh, No, sir," said Arlen. "We were just wondering about that old place. We haven't seen any signs of ghosts up there and we'd be too scared to go inside and look anyway."

"Well, you should probably stay away from that old place. It might be dangerous and you could get hurt. I imagine the wood floors in there are probably in pretty bad shape by now," John said. "Now then, here's your candy bar, Arlen. Do the rest of you boys want any candy to go with that pop?"

"No, we're good," I said. "We just wanted a drink. We'll leave the bottles outside in your cases. Here's a quarter for the candy bar and four bottles of pop."

"Ok," John said. "We'll see you around. Thanks for the business. Try not to get thrown in jail anymore," John was joshing us as we were leaving.

5

Ma was in the kitchen when I got home, starting to prepare supper, and Grandpa was sitting at the kitchen table talking to Ma.

"Well, old timer," Grandpa said. "What brings you home before the cows?"

"Oh, we were just doing boy stuff," I said.

"I saw you out there with your gang of cutthroat thieves, plotting against the world," He joshed.

"Actually our plan to overthrow the world isn't working out too well, so we decided to just have a bottle of pop instead and talk to John about that old house on Market Street."

"Well, John would be the one to talk to. He's been around here most of his life and he's pretty good on local history. What in particular are you looking for?" Ma asked.

"We are still looking for a reason why others are interested in that old house. We've seen three different strangers taking an interest in it, and it's obvious they aren't going to buy it," I said.

"How do you know what someone else is going to do, Lenny?" Ma asked. "Are you sticking your nose into business that doesn't belong to you again? You and your band of 'merry men' need to find more productive things to do with your time. Don't you have some fishing that needs to be done, or lawns that need mowing? I swear, I've got to find you a summer job just to keep you out of trouble. Your imagination is just going to get you into trouble again if you don't tend to your own horses."

"Aww leave the boys alone, Rose," Grandpa chimed in. "They aren't doing anything that any other red-blooded bunch of boys wouldn't do. Life is full of mysteries and boys need to explore."

"Pa, you are always sticking up for him. Why don't you help me discipline him a little instead of always taking his side?"

"It's not a matter of taking sides, Rosy, it's a matter of justice. Let a boy be a boy without riding him for being curious. You raised him right. He knows right from wrong, and if he sees something wrong, it's only natural that he's going to want make it right, or at least find out what's making the world turn."

"Well, I don't know. It just seems like every time his curiosity gets aroused, someone ends up in trouble, or worse, in danger."

"Aww Ma," I said. We're not in any trouble. Just curious to learn about what's going on around us. Somebody has to watch after the neighborhood."

"Well, you aren't the law and it isn't your job to be snooping into other's affairs. If you have a complaint or a concern, tell Deputy Kingsman about it. It's his job to investigate things."

"We don't have anything to offer him but some hunches. When we get more concrete evidence then we'll give it to him and let him settle it, I promise."

"You just stay away from that old house," Ma retorted. "It's a dangerous old building. I don't need you getting hurt from falling through and old rotten flooring or getting into trouble by spying on others."

I knew it was a lost cause so I gave up.

"Ok, Ma, we'll be very careful. But we're just having fun. After all, we are the Woodstock Irregulars and we have to be working on a case all the time."

"Yeah, Ma, don't forget how famous they are," my sister piped in who had been standing at the sink taking it all in. "They might catch an international jewel thief with a big reward and we'll all be rich!"

"Dummy up, Susan. If we need a kidnap victim we'll let you volunteer," I offered.

"Now kids, stop bickering. Let's put an end to this. You just stay out of trouble young man," Ma admonished.

"Rosy, let boys be boys while they still can," Grandpa said. "Just be careful Slim and come to me if you need anything."

"Thanks Grandpa," I said.

I waited for dad to get home from work and asked him if it was OK for the four of us to ride with him to town on Saturday because we wanted to go to the library. As usual it was OK so

I called the other guys and let them know to be at our place by 7AM on Saturday. That gave Dean and me all day Friday to do some biking and fishing and maybe get in some swimming before school started.

Friday arrived and the day went quickly. We made a lot of passes around the block on our bikes to keep an eye on the house, but we didn't expect anything to happen in the middle of the day, and also it was good for the crooks to see us riding around and paying no particular attention to the house so we wouldn't raise their suspicions in case they were watching us. I was pretty sure Larry was up on the hill with binoculars checking us out.

Saturday morning we all met at my place and we piled into Dad's 1954 Nash for the ride to town. Dad stopped at the gas station in Rockbridge to put in a couple dollars of gas and we arrived just before 8AM at the AMC Rambler garage (Nash had changed it's name to Rambler in 1957).

The first thing we did was join Dad in the garage for some coffee and donuts they always had before starting work, but we had pop instead. Fergee, the owner, was in the office doing some paperwork but he ventured out into the showroom to say good morning to everyone and have a cup of coffee with them. When the clock struck eight everyone got up, rinsed out their coffee cups, which all hung in a row on pegs on the wall with names on each of the cups, and John and Herb and Dale and Dad went into the shop and started work. We said our goodbyes and headed up town.

We assembled at the library and discussed our plans. Arlen and Danny were going to dig into the microfiche and look for clues in the past history of Richland County and especially the history of Woodstock.

Dean and I were going to go to the court house and try to find out who owns that old house and maybe try to track down current owners to see what they knew. If we came up with enough information, I wanted to go see Lt. Jake Bower, a friend of Dad's who worked at the local Police Department. I had met Jake several times so we were on pretty good terms and I could ask him questions that might raise an eyebrow from other officers that didn't know me.

We arrived at the court house and went to records.

"Hello boys," the lady at the counter greeted us. "What can we do for you today?"

"Maybe you remember us?" I asked. "We were here earlier this summer to get some information about an old abandoned house in Woodstock."

"Why, yes, I do remember you!" She claimed. "You are the boys that call yourselves 'the Woodstock Irregulars' and you solved a big mail-theft case with the help of some of the information you got from us!"

"Yes, Ma'm," I said. "We are on another case that I can't really talk about yet, but we need more information if you'd be willing to help?"

"I don't see why not. You boys really put Richland Center on the map and I'd be proud to help you any way I can. Are you on the trail of some more thieves, or maybe a good murder mystery?"

"To tell you the truth, we need information on the owner of another piece of property in Woodstock. If I could see a platte map I'll show you which one it is," I told her.

She brought out the same platte map we had used earlier this year and I pinpointed the property. She went to the shelves and pulled a couple ledgers down and took them to her desk. After comparing some information between the two she wrote down somethings on a slip of paper, returned the ledgers to the shelves and came back to the counter.

"Here is all I could find, boys," she said. "It appears that house has been in arrears for taxes for quite a few years now. The first owner was a Rance Hillsboro. The house was built in 1855. Mr. Hillsboro died in 1922 and his estate sold it to Larry Thompson in 1940. Taxes were paid regularly until just about five years ago. As you may know, after seven years we can put it up for auction for back taxes. The last address we had on Larry Thompson was at the Federal Prison in Waupon, Wisconsin.

"We had just seen a strange man around the place acting very suspicious and we were investigating," I informed her.

"I see, another big case, huh? Well, if you find a million dollars, you be sure to let me know, OK?" She kidded us.

"Oh, yes, you'll be able to read about it in the papers again. I can see the headlines now, 'the Woodstock Irregulars' nab another criminal in Woodstock and get a one million dollar reward,' but of course then we'd have to pay taxes!" I laughed. She laughed with us.

It looked like it was time to go see what Lt. Bower was doing. He worked second shift at night from 4pm to midnight so he would be at home most likely.

We headed up on Park St. to locate his house. Jake's squad car was in the driveway so we went to the door and rang the doorbell.

"Well, what do we have here? Woodstock's most famous detectives." He knew all about our first case. "Come on in."

We followed him into his study.

"What's on your mind today, Slim?" Jake asked innocently.

"We might need your help," I said. "We have some information but not all the answers yet, so we are all four in town doing some research. There's an old abandoned house in Woodstock that was built way back in 1855 and it's in pretty bad repair but it belongs to a known criminal."

"Oh, you're talking about the old Hillsboro place," Jake replied. You couldn't pull anything over on him. "Yes, that place used to belong to a guy named Harry Thompson, no, that's not right, just a minute...Larry, Larry Thompson. Last I heard he was in Waupon for some sort of gold theft or something like that. But that was a long time ago, probably back in the 40s or 50s. What's that got to do with the super sleuths?"

"To tell you truth, somebody has been snooping around the place and we were trying to find out who it is. We don't like strangers in our town unless they present themselves and have some sort of official business in town. You know, we have to watch out for each other in those small communities because we are a long ways away from a police department."

"You have Sheriff's deputy Kingsman that lives just down the road from you," Jake replied.

"Yes, and he vowed to help us if we needed it after we broke that last case, but we can tell he still doesn't believe kids that might be telling tall tales to make him look foolish."

"Besides," interjected Dean, "He's more likely to find cause to throw us in jail before we can break the case. He's been really good at that."

"Yes, I see what you mean," Jake said. "He had you in jail twice on that last case, and he was wrong both times. Well, I'm glad you feel you can trust me. I'd never betray your trust on any information you give me. But police work is very serious work and it's also very dangerous. I wouldn't want you to get hurt, so let's start at the beginning and let me hear your story from the start of this investigation. I might be able to help you."

So we started at the beginning and brought Jake up to speed. He sat there and nodded his head as we touched on each point. However, we did skip the part about Larry confronting those other two guys because we didn't want this to look overly-dangerous and have our case taken away from us before we had solved the mystery.

"So far, boys, there's been no crime committed. It's certainly a possibility that Larry has either been paroled or escaped, but I probably would have heard if he had escaped, so we'll give him the benefit of the doubt for now. And just because he hasn't paid the taxes for five years on the house doesn't mean the house isn't still his, so he can do whatever he wants to. I have to admit that there would no reason for him to be sneaking around at night, but you don't have any proof he was the guy you saw in the rain that night. But I have to admit, whoever it was is acting awfully suspicious by camping out on the hill and keeping an eye on the place. I'll tell you what. Let me do some checking on this for you and I'll call you at home in a day or two and let you know what I found out. In the meantime, you boys play it very careful. Just observe. Don't get involved. If it looks like anything dangerous, give me and Deputy Kingsman a call. As a city officer I'm also deputized to work anywhere in the county, but don't overlook the officer that

THE MYSTERY OF THE ABANDONED HOUSE

lives closest to you if time is of an essence."

We thanked Lt. Bower for his help and advice and left to meet with the other guys at the library. Arlen and Danny had been very busy and gathered a lot of information.

"We found out that Larry owns that house, but he hasn't paid taxes on it for five years. Just two more years and it will be sold at auction for back taxes," I told Arlen and Danny.

"And we went to see Lt. Bower," Dean said. "He said that Larry had been in the Waupon Federal Prison for some sort of gold theft. Bower said he might be out by now and he'd do some checking on him for us."

"Just wait till you see what we found," Arlen said. "Larry Thompson was convicted of stealing four bars of gold bullion from a bank he worked at in Milwaukee. Only two bars were found when he was captured. He was tried and sentenced to 20 years and was just recently paroled. It was reported that he had an accomplice, but was never proven and he took the fall all by himself."

"Four bars of gold? How much could that be worth?" Dean asked.

Arlen replied, "I researched that too. A bar of gold weighs 27.4 pounds. I don't know what it was worth back then, but today gold is worth about $35.27 per ounce, so if you do the math, today each of those bars is worth well over $15,000. That means Larry has an idea where over $30,000 in gold is stashed and he's trying to find where, exactly, in that house that paroled guy, Joe, hid it for him and he's trying to be very sneaky about retrieving it so he doesn't get caught with it. I don't think they can try him again on the same charge, but the gold still doesn't belong to him, and he has to return it if he has it in his possession, although I don't know what they could charge him with because he's already paid for his crime. But the gold still belongs to the bank."

"I think they could get him for concealing evidence," I said. "But I don't know what the punishment would be since he's already served his time for stealing it. But the punishment isn't our problem. Making sure the gold is returned is our real case."

"That and the fact we might be able to implicate one or both of the other guys as his partners that escaped punishment," Danny said.

"Yes, that's true," agreed Dean. "They haven't been punished yet. If the gold is discovered, they might have to do their time in prison also. Wow, this is getting into a pretty complicated case. I can just see us going to jail with them for concealing information."

"Stop worrying, Dean," I said. We aren't concealing any information that is worth anything in court. We only have our suspicions, and we've given our suspicions to at least two police officers, Lt. Bower and Danny's brother, so it's not like we've concealed anything. We just have to dig up more information."

"Where do we go from here?" Arlen asked.

"I'm not sure," I said. "The best thing we could do is find the gold, then we'd have the evidence we need to take to the authorities and probably start an arrest. We also need to find where all three of these guys are living at the present so the police will know where to find them if we get enough evidence. So let's start back at the house. We need to sneak in there without being seen and do a better job of looking for a hiding place for the gold."

"And just how do you propose to that?" Dean asked.

"How about with some help?" Danny questioned.

"What kind of help?" I queried.

"Let's get someone, or more than one person, go to the house and look at it like they are thinking about buying it?" Danny replied. "While they are making a spectacle of themselves to attract the attention of the bad guys, we could sneak in from a different direction unnoticed."

"Not a bad idea," I said. "Let's give that one some more thought and planning. But we know that we really need to find the evidence so one way or another we have to spend more time in that house. I think it's time we get back to the Rambler garage and get ready to go back home with Dad where we can work on the problem better."

As we walked out of the library something odd struck me. There was a man standing on the street corner reading a newspaper. Now that might be something you'd see on a busy street in Madison or Milwaukee, or in a movie, but not on an empty street corner in Richland Center. He was dressed all in black with a dress hat and a long black overcoat. He reminded me of the prowler because his clothes looked the same. He glanced over the top of the paper at us and then went back to reading.

When we got a block from the library I said, "Did you guys notice that man standing on the street corner reading a paper?"

Arlen said he saw him, but Dean and Danny said they hadn't noticed.

"Don't you think that's a little strange in Richland Center?" I asked. "And he was dressed almost like the prowler I saw that night in the rain, all in black with a black dress hat and black suit jacket, except the prowler had a black trench coat. I noticed he looked over the top of the paper at us for a second, then appeared to go back to reading."

"Do you think we are being followed," Dean asked.

"I'm not sure, but he certainly looked out of place here in this little town," I replied. "We'd better keep our eyes open and watch for him again. I don't know if the prowler is tailing us or we have someone else on our trail, but there's no such thing as a coincidence."

We hiked back to the garage and hung around for half an hour while we waited for dad to get off work. We got home in time for dinner and Ma had a big pot roast in the oven so she invited all the boys to stay for dinner, and we were pretty hungry by then. We had pot roast, mashed potatoes and gravy, creamed corn, and rhubarb cobbler for desert. Everyone was very stuffed after dinner, so the four of us retired to Dean's office to discuss our next step.

6

"I've been thinking about it and I wonder if Grandpa would be willing to play the decoy?" I pondered.

"It wouldn't hurt to ask," Dean replied.

"What about our sneak attack on the house?" Arlen asked. "Do you have any ideas how to get in unnoticed?"

"I think we could enter the east side to the balcony with a ladder or go through a window at the lower level on the east side or the back of the house. The west side and south side are easy for them to watch. There's no way for them to watch the back side nor the side facing the fort unless they are in the fort," I said. "Grandpa could enter through the front door and pretend to be looking at it like an interested buyer, then he could go through the house and open a window at the rear so we could get in easily."

Everyone agreed that sounded like the most workable solution. I turned to look out the large picture window of Dean's office just in time to see a big black Chevrolet sedan pass by the building.

"Hey, did you guys see that car?" I asked. They had.

"Who in heck was that?" Dean asked.

"I'm sure I don't know," I said, "but it's obvious it doesn't belong in this neighborhood."

We watched out the window and saw it turn left on Woodstock Drive then we lost sight of it until it got to Market street and then turned left again and drove past the old house, then we couldn't see where it went, but it was probably coming back down Wolf Lane. Sure enough, it appeared at the corner of Wolf Lane and Southshore Drive and stopped in the intersection for a while, probably looking around. Then it continued north on Wolf Lane.

"Well I'll be a skinned coon," Danny said. "He sure is looking around."

"Yes, it appears we have another guest in town. The disappearance of the gold and the reappearance of Mr. Thompson seems to be dragging people out of the woodwork," I concluded. But we still didn't know who the new stranger was. We never did see the car very well Sweeny had driven to the house that night, and then got caught in the house by Larry, but it didn't look like a brand new Chevrolet sedan so I thought we had another intruder into our case.

"Well that's just great," Dean complained. "That's all we needed. Another one to watch out for."

"Yes, that does add another complication," I said. "But we won't let it spoil our new plans. I'll go over and have a talk with Grandpa and try to get this set up. You guys hang tight for a few minutes."

I walked over to Grandpas to find him working in the garden.

"Hello, old timer, whatcha got on your mind today besides avoiding lawn mowing?"

"Hi Grandpa, I'm not avoiding law mowing, I'm just waiting for it to grow a little more so I don't waste energy."

Grandpa grinned.

"I've got a lot to tell you, and we need to ask your help."

I told him everything that had transpired. He stood there quietly leaning on his hoe handle. Finally he sat down on the bench that sits at the edge of the garden for purposes of resting while working in the garden and took a drink from a jug of water he had sitting there.

He finally said, "Well, this case is really turning into something. I'd sure hate for your mother to find out about it. That would put a stop to it and you would never know how it all ended. I don't think there's any danger in looking at the house as a prospect for an income property for an old man, do you? So when do you want to do this?"

"Tomorrow is Sunday. How about we do it after we go to church and have dinner?" I asked.

"Sounds like a great idea," he said. So I left and went over to Dean's to tell the guys.

"Sunday afternoon sounds good to me," Dean said. Arlen and Danny agreed. "Let's meet at your grandpa's about 1:30pm." The plan was laid.

The next morning we all went to church. That is, everyone in my family, and Dean went with us. Danny and Arlen would be down by 1:30.

After church we had a large meal at my place, then made our excuses to leave after dinner so we could all assemble at Grandpa's. Grandpa was a little late getting away from Mom, but we were finally all together.

"I'll drive around the block because it looks more official arriving in a car," Grandpa said. "Then I'll spend some time piddling around inspecting the wood trim and the door and windows and the paint. Then I'll go inside and go to the farthest rear or north window, the one least likely to be seen, and unlock it so you can get in. Then I'll go back to the front of the house where I can be seen in the windows and do a lot of inspecting. You guys can come in whenever you want to. I'll be there maybe 15 minutes or so and drive away. The house is all yours, but post a lookout so that no one can sneak up on you while your looking for hiding places for the treasure."

That all sounded like a crackerjack idea so we decided we'd head that way in about 15-20 minutes.

Grandpa pulled out of the drive and drove around the block. We walked back over by Deans and dropped down into the creek bed and started slowly walking south, being very quiet and staying in the tall weeds.

When we got to the house we hunkered down and crept to the northeast rear corner. It looked like Grandpa had finished and left already so we tried the window and it was unlocked. We raised the window and three of us crawled in being very careful to keep away from windows on the front and west sides. We were pretty sure the hiding space would be in the study and it was easy to get to without being seen. Danny stayed outside to watch for anyone approaching the house and he could warn us, hopefully in time to duck back out the window.

We moved into the study and started examining the boards in the floor, very minutely. Very carefully. Looking for any signs of tools used to lift any of the boards. After about ten minutes we had covered the floor very well and didn't find anything. Then we started examining the wainscoting panels but they appeared to have been painted with some heavy paint in the past. That turned out to be a help rather than a hinderance because you could see if the paint was broken where edges join together. I was inspecting one wall, Arlen on another, and Dean on the third wall. After a very careful inspection we had found nothing so we all went to the final wall to finish up, and there it was, right up against the fireplace. One of the panels had the paint broken along all four edges. Now the trick would be to figure out how to remove that paneling without doing any damage.

Arlen and I both had our Barlow jackknives in our pockets so we carefully inserted the large blade along the edge of the panel and tried to carefully pry the panel out. We were very careful not to leave any new marks on anything. We worked all around the panel but couldn't find any way to loosen it. It didn't have any apparent nails or staples in it, but we couldn't figure out what was holding it in place. Just then there were three taps on the rear of the house by the window we came in through so we bolted for the window and climbed out, closing it after us. Danny was waiting there looking very nervous.

"What's up?" I asked.

"There's some guy up at our fort looking this way with binoculars," he said. "I was watching the front of the house for anyone approaching, but I just happened to swing my head around to check all around me for any surprises and I caught movement up at the fort. I moved out of sight, but I could still see the fort. Then I saw the figure move out in the open looking for me again, I assume. He is dressed all in black with a hat and had binoculars in front of his face. As soon as he located me and saw that I was looking right at him, he disappeared."

"Well, we don't know if it's Sweeny, or Larry, or that other guy we saw in town that appeared to be watching us," I said. "He's apparently not interested in coming on down to meet us, so keep an eye on the fort and we'll go back in and see if we can get into a compartment on the wainscot that looks like it's been opened before."

We opened the window and went back in while Danny stood guard again and Dean stayed with him to provide more eyes to watch both directions better.

There had to be some way to get that panel out and determine why it had been removed before.

We went back to the panel and started examining the wainscot around it more carefully, then noticed the wooden buttons on the top of each panel. I tried pressing the buttons but nothing happened, so I twisted the left one and it wouldn't move. Then I twisted the right one and it cranked the panel open a little, so I continued to twist it and the panel kept sliding back until it was open.

"Well, I'll be darned," I said. "There must be a string attached to pulleys that work the sliding door. Wind the string and the door opens."

We got out our penlights and looked inside, but it was just a crawl space.

"Looks like we are going to have to go inside," Arlen said.

"Looks that way. Let's start in and see where it goes."

We crawled into the space and crawled forward. Arlen turned around and manually slid the panel back in place so no one would know where we entered just in case the wrong people came into the house and saw the open panel. We didn't want to help out the bad guys.

Almost as soon as we got fully into the crawlspace, we came to a ladder that went down. It looked sturdy so we climbed down the ladder, about six feet, then we could stand up and walk in the tunnel. Before we had gone about ten feet, there was a small wooden crate on the floor with the lid nailed shut on it. We didn't have any tools to disassemble it so we decided to deal with that on our return trip.

We walked through the tunnel, filled with spider webs and an occasional rat running in front of us. It was very damp down there and I could assume the water table wasn't far below this. It smelled of must and old wet dirt and was a little muddy on the floor. I don't know how far we walked but we were going west from the house. Finally the tunnel came to an end with another ladder going up. I climbed up the ladder.

"Whatcha see up there?" Arlen asked.

"I've come to a wood ceiling, which is a wood floor, I'd guess, of some other place. Let's think about this. We were going west from the house, of that I'm pretty sure. The only place west of the house is the garage for the township grader. I think that's as far as we can go until we go to the garage and examine the floor and look for a trapdoor or something."

So I went back down the ladder and we made our way back to the wood box on the floor. We tried to lift it, but it was too heavy to carry so we left it and returned to the closed panel. We listened for a while for any movement or voices in the house and finally after not hearing anything, I slid the panel open just a crack to look out into the room. Nothing there. So I slid the panel open and we crawled out, closed the panel, and climbed back out the window, closing it after us.

"Did you see any more movement?" I asked Danny.

"Nope, nothing moving anywhere," Danny replied.

"Nothing on the other side of the house either," Dean chipped in, "But we know we were seen by at least one person. So much for doing our searching without being seen!"

"Wait till we tell you guys what we found. Let's get back to the office first to talk about it."

We all headed back down the creek toward Dean's office, but I was thirsty and needed an afternoon snack so we headed to the store first.

"Howdy, young fellers," John said when we came in the door. "You out looking for girls today?"

"Aww shucks, no," I said. "We've got a lot better things to do than that."

"Just wait until your 16," John said. "Then there won't be anything better to do." And he had a hearty laugh.

"We just need an afternoon snack. We get hungry and thirsty about this time of day," I said.

"Well, help yourself. You know what you want."

So we each pulled a bottle of pop out of the flowing ice water in the pop cooler, then Arlen and Danny visited the candy bar shelf but Dean and I went for the ice cream freezer where we each picked out a Fudgsicle. We each laid a dime on the counter.

"What kind of detective work have you guys been up to today?" John asked.

"Well," I said, "we've been tracking old lost gold bullion."

"That's interesting. Do you need any help carrying it?"

"I think we'll figure out some way to move it, but if we need any help, we'll come see ya," I said.

"Ok, well, just don't get caught with it or you'll be back in jail again." And then he had a good laugh over that joshing, but it was getting a little old. "You boys take care and thanks for the business."

We left and took our booty back to Dean's office.

"Well, tell us what happened," Danny said.

"We found the secret to opening a panel in the wainscot. It's one of the wooden buttons sticking out of the top of the wainscot trim right next to the fireplace. You just twist it and it rolls up a string that slides the panel door open. Then we crawled inside and closed it behind us and then we came to a ladder that went down about 6 feet to a tunnel. In the tunnel we found a wooden box with the lid nailed shut so we couldn't see what was in it, but it's heavy, very heavy. I think it's the gold bullion that still missing."

"Holy cow," said Danny and Dean together.

"Why didn't you bring it out with you?" Dean asked.

"First of all, the tunnel goes farther, then we came to another ladder. I climbed it but it had a wood board ceiling with I deduced was the flooring in the old grader garage. There was no way to exit the tunnel there, so we backtracked and tried to lift the box, but it was too heavy, so we left it until we could figure out how to get into the tunnel from the grader garage and that way we could sneak it out even if someone was watching the house."

"That's a great idea," said Danny. "The first thing we need to do then is go up to the garage tomorrow, Monday, when the grader is gone to work and look for a way to locate the opening. I wonder what's the best way to find it?"

"The easiest way is to crawl back into the tunnel from the house," I said, "then make some noise on the wooden ceiling and you guys locate the sound and try to draw out a square on the wood floor with a pencil so we can figure out how to cut the planks if there's not some sort of trap door that's just locked in the garage. But first we'll all go together to the garage and look for a trap door. It would save us a lot of time and work if we can find an easy way in."

It was now supper time so we split up and made plans to meet at the garage about 10AM in the morning. In the meantime, right after supper, Dean and I would go to the fort and keep an eye on the house until dark.

7

We watched the house until dark, then gave up and went home. No one was brave enough to go near it with so many guys watching it. We felt the treasure was safe for at least one more night and if we had any luck at all, we'd have it in our possession tomorrow morning.

I awoke Monday morning with a brilliant sun in the sky. The light breeze from the east was bringing the fragrance of the morning glories into the house. Robins, meadowlarks and wrens were all singing their own tunes to a glorious day. I quickly dressed and sauntered into the kitchen for some breakfast. Ma was in the utility room with the old wringer washer getting loads ready for the clothes line today. Monday was always wash day.

"Grab yourself a bowl of Rice Krispies for breakfast. There's a bowl of sugar on the table," Ma hollered from the utility room. "I'll fix you a nice dinner but I have to get this wash out on the line while the sun is shining bright."

I went to the cupboard and grabbed the Rice Krispies, some milk from the refrigerator, a bowl and a glass for milk and sat down for breakfast. I liked Rice Krispies, but they really needed a lot of sugar to give them any flavor.

After breakfast I rinsed my bowl and glass and put them in the sink and headed over to Dean's.

As I walked into the shop, Mr. Brewster was busy working on the rewind rope on a lawn mower.

"A dillar a dollar a ten o'clock scholar, you used to come at nine o'clock and now you come at noon," he recited an old nursery rhyme.

"It's not noon yet," I said. "But if you work any slower on that mower it will be." joshing worked both ways.

"Aww shucks, I finished this hours ago. I'm just doing it over again for practice," he kidded. "Jungle Jim is in his office," He said.

I walked into the office and there was Dean, sitting in his favorite office chair behind his oversize desk, trying to look important.

"Is there anything I can help you with, kid?" Dean questioned in his foolish fashion.

"Naw, I just wanted to talk to the man in charge but all I see is a little boy sitting at a man's desk trying to sound important."

"At least I've got a desk to look important at," Dean defended.

"Ok, I surrender. The other guys should be here soon. Arlen is usually early and Danny is usually late. I had an idea," I said.

"I'll bet it died of loneliness," Dean teased me.

"No, what I had was the thought that if the gold is in that box, and I'm pretty sure it is, we should remove the gold and replace it with something to fool the thieves. We don't want them know the gold is missing as soon as they find an empty box. That would put the blame on us and they might come looking for us."

"What did you have in mind?"

"Your dad has those ingots of lead that he melts down to make bullets and wheel weights and other things. He always keeps several on hand. A bar of lead weighs 25 pounds and that's almost the same weight as an ingot of gold at 27 pounds."

"27.4 pounds," Dean corrected me.

"Ok, let's round that off to the nearest pound, so 27 pounds is close enough. Very few people can tell the difference in 2 pounds. I think we should borrow a couple of bars of lead, paint them gold with the spray paint you have on the shelf, and substitute them. It might buy us some time to help the law catch the crooks in the act, but we won't risk them getting away with the real gold."

"You know? That's a real good idea. Why didn't I think of that?"

"Because all you think about is fishing."

"Speaking of which, we haven't been fishing for a week now, you've kept us so busy with this case," Dean complained.

"Yeah, I know. I'd like to go fishing too, but I feel this is a lot more important right now. School will be starting in another week and we can always fish after school for several more months before it gets too cold."

"Too cold for you, you mean," Dean said. Dean liked to go ice fishing and I wasn't very crazy about sitting on the ice freezing while waiting for a fish to grab my bait. I hated cold weather.

Just then Arlen came in followed by Danny.

"You guys ready to go?" Arlen asked.

"Almost," I said, then I told them the plan I had devised with the lead ingots. So we went into the garage and asked Mr. Brewster if we could borrow a couple ingots of lead.

"What in tarnation do you need lead ingots for?" Mr. Brewster asked.

"We are going to pretend they are gold ingots and one of us will hide them and the rest will try to find them. It's a great game," I grinned as I stretched the truth.

Mr. Brewster grinned back. He knew something was up, but he didn't want to spoil the fun, so he went in the back room and came out with two bars. We took them outside with a can of gold spray paint and carefully painted the bottoms, waited about 10 minutes for the fast drying lacquer paint to dry, then rolled them over and painted the tops and sides. They looked just like gold ingots. 25 pounds each was a pretty good load for young boys to carry but we carried them up the creek, staying hidden in the weeds. When we got almost to the back of the house between the house and the grader's garage, we saw two men climbing in through the window of the house. We ducked down farther into the tall grass.

"Oh, now look what we've gotten into," Dean complained.

"It looks like Sweeny and his partner," I said. "They found the window we left unlocked and they're sneaking in to resume their search without Larry seeing them enter."

"What should we do now?" Arlen asked.

After a little thought I said, "We'll exit the other direction to the grader's garage and go in the back door of the garage. They'll never see us because they will be searching the east side of the house. I just hope we can get to the gold before they discover the secret panel."

We exited the creek behind the grader's garage. The back door was always unlocked so we sneaked in the back and piled the lead bars in the corner. However, we had forgotten that the floor of the garage was covered in gravel. That was going to make it a lot harder to find the entrance to the tunnel.

"Dean, run back home and bring a flat shovel so that we can remove some of this gravel from the floor once we determine where the entrance is. Oh, and bring a small crowbar or nail-puller also. I want to open the wooden box in the tunnel and remove what's in it, hopefully the gold ingots, and replace them with the lead ones. We'll nail the lid shut and leave it right where we found it. We'll also need a small hammer to drive the nails back in."

Dean sneaked back out the door and down the creek. He'd be back in a few minutes.

"What about the guys in the house?" Danny asked.

"I'm not sure," I said. "We'll have to play it by ear. Hopefully they'll give up and leave shortly. What I wouldn't give to be hiding behind that panel in the study right now so I could hear what they're saying."

We looked around the garage for any clues in the gravel of a trap door but didn't find anything. Pretty soon Dean returned with all the tools we needed.

"Well, this isn't going to do us any good if we can't get into the tunnel to help find the entrance in the garage," Dean said.

"That's true," I replied. We have to try to figure out how to get those guys out of the house. I think I have a plan. I'll go down to Grandpa's and ask him to drive up outside the house and honk the horn. That ought to make them nervous enough to rush back out the window and take off. If they don't leave, I'll signal Grandpa to go knock on the door, but I don't want him to enter because they might have guns."

Everyone agreed on the plan and I took off down the creek to Grandpa's place. When I got there, Grandpa was sitting on the porch smoking his pipe.

"Hi Old-timer," Grandpa greeted. "What's on your mind today?"

"Grandpa," I said. "We need a favor. There's two strangers in that house. We don't know what they are doing, but we need to scare them off so they don't interfere with our investigation. We'd like you to drive around the block, stop in front of the house and blow your horn. That should scare them into exiting back out the rear window we saw them climbing into. We'll be in the old grader's garage next door where we are doing some investigating trying to find a connection with that house. One of us will watch the rear window of the house from the garage. If they don't exit, I'll signal you to go knock on the door, but don't go in. We don't know if they have guns."

"This is getting real exciting. I needed something to do this morning. I'll be glad to help you out. You know that if you find the any treasure, it won't belong to you, don't you?"

"Yes, we know that, and we aren't interested in finding anything for ourselves. We want to catch some crooks, that's our only motive."

"OK, as long as you understand the right and wrong."

"I do, Grandpa. You know me better than that."

"Yes, I do. Let's get going. You head back up there and I'll be up after I give you enough time to get back to the garage."

I ran back up the creek to the garage. Pretty soon I heard Grandpa's car coming around the corner. Dean was standing at the back door of the garage looking out at the back of the house so we could tell if Sweeny and his pal exited the house. Grandpa pulled up in front of the house, on the wrong side of the road so that his car horn would be as close as he could get to the house. He let out two long blasts. Waited. Then let out two more.

Dean came running back inside and said, "You should have seen how fast those guys left the house. They cut up behind Wilbur Braithwaite's place and disappeared when they got to Wolf Lane. They probably left their car up there, I'd guess."

I signaled to Grandpa that everything was OK and he drove away. Then Dean and I went to the back of the house, climbed in the window that the two guys had left open, went into the study and opened the panel (it was obvious they didn't have time to find the panel yet). Then we crawled inside, closed the panel and made our way down the ladder to the tunnel and then to the wooden box. It was still there, undisturbed. Then we made our way to the exit ladder, climbed up and and started pounding on the ceiling. Pretty soon I heard Danny's voice.

"Can you hear me?" Danny asked, but not too loud to be heard outside.

"Yes, we hear you," I said. See if you can locate the edges of the this opening and make a line in the gravel with the shovel to try to outline approximately where the opening is."

I then started tapping the wood board ceiling with the butt of my Barlow knife until I had gone all the way around the opening.

"I think we have a good line," Danny reported quietly back down to us. "Come on back."

We left the tunnel, crawled back through the panel in the study, closed the panel, back out the window and across the creek to garage. When we went in the garage we saw a nice square drawn in the gravel.

"That looks great, guys," I complimented them. We took the shovel and cleared off the gravel in the square. Then we cleared it back another foot on each side. Zero. No trap door.

"Well, that sure puts a crimp in this bullion rescue attempt," Arlen said.

"Yes, I agree, it sure does, but I had a backup plan already worked out," I said. We'll get a brace and bit and drill a large hole in the wood, then take a keyhole saw and cut out two boards over the ladder. We can replace them later. It's only a minor setback."

"Why don't we just rescue the gold bullion through the house entrance and carry it back to the garage?" Dean asked.

"We could do it that way," I replied, "But I think it's necessary to have an entrance in the garage to connect the two buildings. This would give us an emergency exit in case we are ever trapped in the tunnel. We just as well make the tunnel entrance in the garage now and do everything from this side so we don't have to go into the house anymore, which is more dangerous." Everyone agreed that this sounded reasonable.

Since Dean's dad had the tools we needed, he could go get them, but then we might have more explaining to do. In my dad's garage I knew where his brace and bits were hanging as I had used them a lot, so I volunteered to run home and get what we needed. I ran back down the creek being sure to stay hidden in the weeds. It was Monday and Dad would be at work all day, so there'd be no one around our garage to question me. The front doors were open, as Dad left the garage open all the time, and I just walked in and grabbed the brace and large hole saw bit, but I had a heck of a time finding the keyhole saw. I finally found it on a shelf over the workbench and headed back to the grader's garage with the tools.

When I got back we determined where the ladder would be and I used the hole saw bit and drilled a large hole in the first board. The perfectly round wood from the hole stuck in the bit so we pulled the wood block out of the bit and laid it aside. Then it was easy work to cut across two boards, carefully so as not to cut the beams under them. Then I used the hole saw bit and drilled a hole in the other end and saved the wood block again, and we sawed across the other end of the two boards, however, they didn't drop down the hole because the boards were laid across the wood beams which I had been careful not to cut. We picked up the boards and there was plenty of room to fit our slender bodies between the 24" inch centers of the cross-beams.

"That worked really slick," Arlen said.

"Yeah, really slick for a burglar and break and entry," Dean complained. "If this doesn't lead to another jail term, I'll be really surprised."

"At least you'll be with friends," I said to cheer him up. It didn't work.

8

Dean was too nervous to get involved moving the gold bullion, so we left him in the garage as a lookout. Arlen, Danny and I took the two lead ingots down the ladder and laid them on a shop rag we found in the garage, then went back up and got the small crowbar and hammer and carried them down the ladder. With our penlights we walked back into the dank and dark musty smelling tunnel toward the wooden box. Unfortunately it was a tell-tale sign that we had been down there because of all the broken spiderwebs, so we decided to clear out all the spiderwebs to make it look like there never were any there. Nobody ever notices what *isn't* there. They only notice if something's been disturbed or looks out of place.

We got to the box and used the crowbar to lift the nailed-down boards on top of the box. There they were. Two beautiful pristine gold ingots. Fifty-four pounds worth. $30,000 in 1960 money, but they would have been worth a lot less in 1940 money.

"Ok, guys, it's payday. We found what we were looking for," I said. "Let's carry these back to the ladder and bring the lead ingots back here, put them in the box and nail the boards back on."

"What about all the tracks we've made in the muddy floor?" Arlen asked.

"Good question," I said. "Lets get this gold out of here and the lead ingots secure in the box, then we need to carefully try to wipe out or obscure our footprints. Odds are, if they ever find the secret entrance, they'll not be looking for other footprints and they'll be so excited at finding the wooden box that they'll grab it and run without looking around. But in case they do look around, like maybe go to the end of the tunnel, we've got to secure the opening we just made in the garage so they'll be forced to go back the way they came. It might help in their capture and arrest if they are caught coming out of the tunnel back into the house, but catching them in the act and having law enforcement here at the right time is going to be the tricky part."

So we carried the gold to the ladder and brought the lead back, put it in the box, and nailed the boards back in place. Then we took a heavy rug from the garage and a rag and we went back through the tunnel to the ladder from the house. I climbed up the ladder with a rag and wiped down all footprints behind the panel and down the ladder. We took the rug and drug it behind us down the tunnel which smoothed out all the footprints in the muddy floor. When we got to the ladder into the garage, we took the gold ingots up the ladder and then I carefully wiped off all evidence of mud on the ladder. Now it was an easy fix to put the two boards back on the beams and nail them down good and solid. Only the two holes I had drilled in the boards offered any clue and we'd figure out how to hide those holes. After looking around the garage we found a box of 10 penny nails, so we nailed the boards in place. I would like to have made a trap door in case we ever needed to use the tunnel in the future, but we didn't have time to fabricate one right now. The two holes were still a problem, until I remembered the two wooden circles that came out of the holes when I drilled them. We grabbed the two round wooden circles I had drilled out, but they were too loose to stay in the holes, however a few brad nails around the edge of each one made them tight enough to not be noticed. Mission accomplished, except what to do with the gold now.

We figured the last place anyone would look for gold would be in that old garage. Remember the old adage, "hide in plain sight." So we got a ladder from the corner and climbed up to a beam about 10 feet off the floor and laid the ingots on that beam. Then we brushed dust off beams on the other side of the garage into a dustpan and used that to dust the the ingots so they wouldn't be recognizable. From the floor you couldn't even see them and no evidence that anyone had even been up there. Perfect in every way. I put the ladder back where I found it.

Now it was time to go back to work catching the bad guys. I felt the hard part was done. If all else went wrong, we could still return the gold along with descriptions of the guys involved and the cars they drove. But the finishing touch would be to have the law catch them in the act. The gold was safe.

"Ok, the gold is safe," Dean said. "What's the next step. We want to see these guys behind bars."

"Yes, that's the whole plan," I said. "We now have to devise a plan to catch them, but we've got time on our side now. Let's go to the office and return all our tools to my dad's garage and Dean's dad's tools. We'll work on a plan later but for now I want to get out of here and go where it's safe for a while."

We picked up all our tools and used the shovel to put gravel back over the floor where we had removed the two boards so the place would just like it did when we found it. Then we sneaked back down the creek to Dean's place while I detoured to take Dad's tools back to the garage. When I got to Dean's, they weren't there, so I walked across the road to the store.

"I knew I'd find you guys here," I said.

"All that hard work made us hungry and thirsty," Arlen said.

"Well, its almost dinner time. Grab a bottle of pop and we'll go to my place for dinner. Ma always makes plenty."

We bid John farewell and with a bottle of pop each we walked over my place.

"Hi Ma," I said as we walked into the kitchen. "Got enough food for four hungry wayfarers?" I asked.

"There's always plenty of food for growing boys," Ma replied. "What great adventures have you boys been up to all morning?" She asked.

"We discovered gold bullion," I said. "We plan on melting it down into bullets for our hunting rifles." It made no difference what I told her, she wouldn't believe a word of it anyway.

"Oh, that's nice. Maybe you could make a nice ring for me?"

"Sure Ma, if we can get permission from the Treasury Department," I said.

Her curiosity was appeased knowing that boys have great imaginations and we were keeping busy without getting into any trouble.

Ma had pork chops for dinner with chopped fried potatoes and, yuck, green beans. But we did have fresh apple pie for desert with ice cream. After dinner Arlen and Danny decided to split for home. We had done all we could do as a team and now it was watch and wait. Dean and I could do all the watching we needed without camping out. I could see the rear of the house from our upstairs window. The first room of the upstairs was mine to do my electronics work and my soldering without stinking up the house and hear my aardvark sister complaining. I also had a large steamer trunk that I stored my comics collection in and I had my 5-band shortwave radio, that I built from a kit, and a long wire antenna out the window to a willow tree by the creek. I also had my CW radio (Continuous Wave, or morse code) all set up in the corner next to the window and my vertical antenna outside that I used to talk to Arlen. It was my "Bat-Cave." The second room upstairs, facing north, was used for a storage room. Dad had his old wind-up RCA phonograph in there that he'd get out about once a year and play some old 78 RPM records. He also stored his red plaid hunting jacket, cap and pants and insulated rubber boots that he used for deer hunting. There were many boxes of other things that I never knew what was in them. Then there was a trap door in the corner that led into another portion of the attic that didn't have a floor in it so you had to walk on the beams. There was one light bulb in the center of the ceiling with a pull-string on it to light up the area. You couldn't stand up in this area and I don't even know what all my parents stored in there.

There was a vent in the floor of the second room so you could get some heat up into the upstairs when the kerosene stove in the living room downstairs was running, but it was a very limited supply of heat. The walls were all plaster-over-lathe and it was cracking badly and needed to be re-plastered. But the upstairs was my getaway room and I loved the solitude.

I brought dads binoculars from the storage room, hanging with his hunting clothes, and put them by the south-facing window in my room to help keep an eye on the abandoned house. Dean stayed with me after dinner and we went upstairs to read some comics and watch the house. I worked a little on a couple of projects I had started earlier. I had some plans out of the Popular Science magazine for building a tiny morse code, or CW, for Continuous Wave, transceiver that Arlen and I could carry in our pockets. It took very few pieces and looked very easy to solder together. I had just received all the parts I needed from Radio Shack a couple days ago but we had been way too busy to get back to the project, so I worked on it a little at a time. Dean had finally shown an interest in ham radio so I was going to build one for him and Arlen. Dean could at least listen to us, but he couldn't transmit without a license which I hoped he'd commit himself to studying for over the winter when the bad weather kept us locked up inside.

We watched the back of the house off and on the rest of the day, then gave up. Dean went home for supper and I continued to absorb myself in my hobbies in the upstairs room where I could watch for flashlights in the old house after it got dark. About nine o'clock I gave up, and read one of my favorite books for a while that I had started several days ago. It was a boys mystery series by August Derleth who lived in Sac Prairie, Wisconsin. Then I went to bed.

The next morning I was up early and had some toast with a boiled egg sliced-up on it for breakfast. Then the phone rang. It was Lt. Bower.

"Slim? Is that you?" Lt. Bower asked.

"Yes, it is. What did you find out?"

"All I learned is that Larry Thompson had served his time and was now walking the streets somewhere. He supposedly has a house in Milwaukee, but we know he's actually in this area. We have a description of his car but so far he hasn't broken any laws that we know of, so I guess it's up to the Woodstock Irregulars to keep an eye on him. The bank is still missing two of those four stolen gold bullion bars, so there's a reward for their return if they are ever found. But just observe. If he's doing anything illegal, get in touch with Deputy Kingsman or me so we can arrest him."

I agreed we would and thanked him for his help.

I left the house and walked up the creek toward the abandoned house. I cut over to the grader garage and Harry was already out with the grader for the day so the garage was empty again. I opened up the step ladder and climbed up so I could see the gold bullion on the beam in the corner of the garage and they were still intact. The floor of the garage looked perfect yet; the gravel all looked undisturbed.

I heard a car coming so I hid behind the garage door and watched the road. Larry Thompson was cruising around the block in his black and white Rambler. He drove by very slowly and carefully watched the house. He disappeared around the block. Pretty soon I heard the car coming again. It drove by slowly again, then disappeared around the block. The third time he stopped in front of the house, apparently convinced that Sweeny and his partner were not there and he was feeling brave. I stayed in the garage and peeked out the window on the east side to watch for movement in the house. I couldn't see anything so I figured he was in the study, still searching for the hiding space. Then I heard another car. I watched out the front garage door and that black Chevrolet sedan drove by slowly. He was eyeing Larry's car, then he drove on by and turned right up by the fort and the car was out of sight. I kept watching. Pretty soon I saw a man dressed in black climb the grader ditch up to our fort, where he stood in the weeds with binoculars, watching the house. I didn't know what to do. I couldn't leave out the front door of the garage without being seen by him, and I didn't want to leave by the back door and risk being seen by Larry in the Study, so I was stuck here for a while, watching and waiting.

I think Larry had heard the car drive by because shortly afterward, he came to the front door. There wasn't any use in sneaking out the back because he knew his car had been seen, however he didn't know if it was Sweeny, but he was now nervous. He stuck his head out the door and looked around cautiously. Of course he couldn't see the stranger with the binoculars so he nervously went to his car and drove away. Shortly after he drove off and turned north on Wolf Lane, the black sedan went down

Wolf Lane the same direction. The crisis was over and I could go home, but I was wishing I could get the license number of that black sedan. I knew Larry didn't have time to find anything with the interruption, so we still didn't have anything on him yet. The plan was to catch them all in the house after they discovered the secret hiding place and recovered the counterfeit bars, then the police could step in and arrest them. We could have helped them find the moveable panel by leaving it open a little bit, but that would have tipped them off that someone had found it before them and they would have gotten suspicious.

I went straight to Dean's office and he was inside assembling an airplane model from balsa wood and tissue. The room smelled of glue and dope for the tissue.

"Hey, I was just up at the garage checking on the gold and Larry drove by three times and stopped, then went in the house. He wasn't in there very long until that black sedan drove by slowly, which spooked Larry. The guy in the black sedan parked out of sight up the hill near the fort, then went to the fort and was watching the house with binoculars. Larry must have heard his car drive by so he came to the door and looked out cautiously then got in his car and left. The guy in the black sedan followed him down Wolf Lane. I don't know what's up, but something's in the wind. I'm going to call Arlen to come down and we'll do some more watching. Also I have his pocket radio finished so I want to give that to him."

"I'd sure like to know who that guy in the black sedan is," Dean said. "We never saw Sweeny's car in the daylight so we don't know for sure it's not him."

"That's true, but the guy in the black sedan is always alone, so I don't think it's Sweeny."

I gave Arlen a call and told him to take a break and come visit us. I didn't tell him that I had his radio finished. That was going to be a surprise gift.

Dean and I got on our bikes and rode around the neighborhood while waiting for Arlen to arrive. He'd be here in half an hour. We rode around the block past the house several times trying to look innocent of anything going on. We rode up the road past the fort toward Dewey Brown's rental farm, looking for the black sedan, but it wasn't around. We turned around and rode down past the church on Wolf Lane and didn't see anything suspicious, so we rode back past the store and out toward Kingman's place and didn't see anything. Finally we rode up toward Dewey Brown's current farm so we could look up on Elephant Foot rock but we couldn't see anything except a little smoke from a small fire. We decided to ride up Southshore Drive to Main Street and head up the hill toward the backside of the rock where we'd seen Larry's car before.

When we got to the top of the hill, there was Larry's car, and another car we didn't recognize. It was a dark colored Studebaker. It's possible that was Sweeny's car.

"Looks like something is going on," Dean said.

"Yes, either Larry and Sweeny are going to shoot it out, or they are going to work out their differences and team up, but it's a pretty good bet that Studebaker is Sweeny's car," I said. "I think we'd better get set for some action. Arlen should be arriving any minute."

We went back to Dean's office and waited. A few minutes later Arlen pulled in.

9

Arlen came walking in the office, "What's up guys?"

"We just saw Larry's car up on the hill and there was another car we didn't recognize, a dark Studebaker. I'm betting it belongs to Sweeny," I said.

"Holy cow. What do you think they're doing? Do you think they are going to have a shootout?" Arlen asked.

"It's possible, but they could also be joining forces," I said. "We think something is in the works and either one or both of them will be visiting the house to try to find the secret panel. We need to be watching them. Arlen, here is a low power CW transceiver I built for you. I have one in my pocket too. It might make a good emergency radio. When it's on 'receive' the 9 volt transistor radio battery should last at least a week." Arlen was really surprised.

"Wow, did you build this?" He asked?

"Yes, I had plans from a Popular Science magazine and I ordered the parts from Radio Shack. It was really simple. It's only 100 milliwatts but under the right conditions and a good outside antenna, it will transmit over 4000 miles, but with this telescoping antenna that's built-in, we can probably only get a couple miles. There's also a wire with an alligator clip that you can use to clip onto anything metal like a rain gutter to give you a bigger antenna, and here's an earphone for listening."

"Wow, what a great idea," he said. "Thanks a lot."

"Ok, here's the plan, Dean and I need to get to the house before those guys come down, and I think they'll be down today to combine efforts to find the hidden panel, if my hunch is right. We'll hide upstairs so we can hear what they are saying through the floor vent. You stay here and monitor the radio. When the time is right, I'll signal you with an SOS and you call Deputy Kingsman. If he doesn't answer, here's LT. Bower's phone number, but it will take him a long time to get here."

Dean and I took off for the house. We went in the rear window, closed it, and went upstairs to wait for the anticipated action.

We sat there all morning and missed dinner.

"I sure would like to go get something to eat," Dean complained.

"So would I," I said, "but this might be our big break. We'll have to stick it out all day and wait for them."

And we did. We waited all afternoon until the sun started setting.

"Geez, I really thought they'd show up today," I apologized. "I wonder what happened at their meeting?"

"Maybe they killed each other," Dean suggested.

"Anything is possible," I said. "But we'd better get home for supper before our parents start worrying."

We left the house and went back to Dean's.

"So I guess nothing happened," Arlen surmised.

"Not a thing, and I was so sure this was going to be our big break. And right now we don't know if Sweeny and Larry made a deal or killed each other. Let's take a quick bike ride up the hill and see if the cars are still there before we go home for supper. Did you get any dinner today?"

"I went to the store and bought a sandwich from the refrigerator and a bottle of pop. I had my radio with me in case you called."

"Great, I'm glad you figured out how to get some food. We didn't think to take any with us and we are really hungry," I replied.

"Boy are we ever," Dean complained. "You and your hare-brained schemes!"

"Ok, neither of us thought to take a lunch. We are both to blame for that," I retaliated.

So we took off on our bikes and five minutes later we could see both cars still in the same place. We turned around and headed back to Dean's.

"Whatever happened today didn't include searching for treasure," Dean said.

"I've got to get home," Arlen said. "Do you want me to come back tomorrow morning?"

"Yes, make it early, say 8AM. We'll pick up our stake-out where we left off. They're getting ready to do something, we just don't know what yet, but I'll bet it's going to be soon, so we'll try again tomorrow. And bring your pocket radio with you and listen for my call."

Then we split up and went home for supper.

"Well, where have you been all day?" Ma asked as soon as I came in the door. "We've already eaten but I still have some warm food in the oven for you."

"Thanks, Ma," I said. "We got busy with our boy-stuff and forgot all about the time. Arlen came down and we were busy all day."

"I'm surprised your stomach didn't interrupt you. I've never known you to miss a meal," Ma said.

"We were getting pretty hungry but you know we often go to the store for a snack to sustain us when we are busy." Which wasn't a lie, but today we had forgotten to pack a snack, which I was going to make sure to remedy tomorrow.

I had supper then went upstairs to keep an eye on the house for a while and watch for flashlights. I fell asleep at my workbench and woke up about 1 AM. I went to the window and looked out at the old house, but there was no sign of activity, so I went to bed.

I was up bright and early the next morning, got dressed, had a bowl of cereal for breakfast and headed over to Dean's place. As soon as I crossed the bridge I could hear a blue jay screaming up a storm farther up the creek. He was near the old house and I knew he was scolding someone for being there. I rushed into the office and Dean wasn't there, so I went out in the shop. There he was, assembling an old lawn mower engine.

"Where's your dad?" I asked.

"He had to go to town so I'm helping out."

"Let's head up to the old house. There's a blue jay screaming at someone messing around up there."

"Let me wash the grease off my hands, first," Dean replied.

He cleaned up and we headed up the creek. When we got to the rear of the house we sneaked under the windows.

"I'll go around to the east side by the study," said Dean.

"Ok, I'll watch the rear window where they enter. If you see anything in the study come back and tell me. That blue jay indicated someone is around here somewhere."

Dean went around to the east side and sidled up to the rear window. Pretty soon I heard someone talking, but it wasn't inside. It was outside on the east side of the house. I sneaked to the corner of the house and peeked around. Dean was in trouble. Sweeny's partner had sneaked up on him.

"Well, look what we have here," the man said as he grabbed Dean by the shoulder. Dean looked like he was going to have a heart attack. "Just what are you doing snooping around out here? OK, brat let's go inside." And he marched Dean around to the front door. This didn't look good. I got my telegraph transmitter out of my pocket, raised the antenna and called Arlen, di di dit, dah dah dah, di di dit three times (SOS, SOS, SOS). C A L L D E P U T Y. Which I repeated three times. I got back a "K" (Dah di dah) from Arlen. I figured it was time to bring in the law.

I watched through the window and could hear them questioning Dean. I couldn't hear what Dean said, but I saw him point to the hidden panel. That was good. I had a plan. Besides, we wanted them to find the panel so we could trap them anyway.

Larry and Sweeny went over to the panel. The third guy grabbed Dean and pushed him toward the cellar door which he unlocked with the key that was already in the lock and pushed Dean inside, then he locked the door.

It didn't take Larry and Sweeny long to figure out how to open the panel. I assume that Dean had told them about the wooden button that you turn to open the panel. The panel opened and they all crawled inside. I couldn't see them now and I knew they had descended the ladder. I quickly climbed in the rear window and ran into the study. I crawled into the panel opening and went to the ladder, then I pulled the ladder up and slide it behind me, and I exited through the panel door. Just as I poked my head out the door into the study, a large hand grabbed me and jerked me to my feet. It was the man from the black sedan with a gun in his hand!

"Slim Lorens, I presume," he said. "I'm Agent Mason from the US Treasury Department." He put his gun away and showed me his badge and ID.

Just then Deputy Kingsman burst into the room, gun drawn.

"Police. Hands up," He ordered.

The Treasury Agent put his hands over his head and turned to face the deputy.

"Let me show you my ID," he said as he held it out for the deputy to see. Kingsman took a step forward and looked at, then put his gun away.

"What's going on here? I got a call from a young man telling me there was an emergency here," Kingsman said.

"Would you like to tell him what happened, young Master Lorens?" Mr. Mason said.

"They've kidnapped my friend, Dean Brewster and now I've trapped those three guys in the tunnel through that open panel. They are rescuing two gold bars of bullion that was stolen 20 years ago. I pulled up the ladder so they couldn't get out until you could get here, but I didn't know there was a Treasury Agent on the case too. Dean is locked in the cellar, we should let him loose," I said.

THE MYSTERY OF THE ABANDONED HOUSE

"You go get him," Kingsman said. "We'll deal with the accused."

I went to the cellar door and unlocked it. Dean was standing at the top of the steps and he was looking very shook up.

"It's about time," he said. "Where are the bad guys?"

"They are about to be arrested," I said. "There's a US Treasury Agent here along with Deputy Kingsman."

"A US Treasury Agent? Holy Cow. How'd he get involved?"

"I have no idea," I said. I just got here myself and he hasn't told us his story yet. As soon as I saw that man grab you, I got on the pocket radio and telegraphed Arlen and told him to call the deputy. The three men found the trick to opening the panel and went inside. As soon as they did, I crawled in the window, went in the open panel and pulled up the ladder to trap them down there. Now the officers have to try to get them out."

After putting the ladder back in place the US Treasury Agent hollered, "Come on out with your hands up. If you have any weapons, you'd better leave them behind. If I see a weapon, I'll shoot first and ask questions later."

We waited. And waited. Another call went out to the bad guys. Still no show.

"What do you think they're doing?" Kingsman asked the Treasury Agent.

"It's hard to say, but they are definitely not coming up without some help. We are going to have to go down there and corner them, I guess."

"Wait a minute," I said. "There's another entrance. That tunnel goes over to the garage next door. We nailed the entrance shut, but you can pull the nails and come at them from both ends."

"That sounds like a great idea," Kingsman and Mason agreed.

So Kingsman stayed behind to watch the open panel in the house and we took Mason over to the garage to show him the other entrance. But when we got there we discovered why they had not come out. They had knocked the boards loose and came up into the garage and escaped. Mason went down into the tunnel while we went next door to the house to tell Kingsman to meet him in the tunnel and we went back to the garage.

After about 10 minutes they both came up into the garage.

"Do you boys know if the gold bullion was in that tunnel?" Agent Mason asked. "There's an empty wooden box on the floor of the tunnel."

"It wasn't an empty box when we last left it," I said.

Then it all added up. "It appears they used the heavy gold bars as a battering ram to knock the boards loose in the garage," Mason said.

"But there's one thing we should tell you," I said.

"Yes," said Dean. "They didn't use the gold bars to break the boards out with."

"What do you mean?" Mason asked.

"Well, you see, we had already taken the bars out for safe keeping so they couldn't escape with them. We thought you'd be able to catch them with some fake bars we left in their place. We painted lead bars with gold paint, which weigh almost as much as a gold bar, and placed them in the box and nailed the lid shut. They used the fake bars to bust the boards out."

"Then where are the real ones?" Mason asked.

"They are right above your head," Dean said, as I got the ladder and moved it under the bars.

"They are right up there on the beam, covered with dust. Hiding in plain sight," I said.

Mason went up the ladder and let out a whistle. Then he handed them down, one at a time, to Deputy Kingsman.

"Well, it appears they outsmarted us and escaped. But thanks to you boys, they outsmarted themselves, too, because they only escaped with lead bars. I wonder how long it will take them to figure out they are lead?"

"Aren't you going to go after them?" I asked

"We would if we knew how they got away and where they went," Kingsman said. "As it is, we don't don't know if they had cars hidden a short distance from here and are already miles away, or if they are cutting cross-country by foot. Any way you look at it, we don't know where to start looking."

"The first place I'd start would be in the rocks up on Elephant Foot." And I turned and pointed at the rocks. "They've been camping up there. The easiest way to get there is go down Woodstock Drive, turn left on Southshore Drive, then turn left at the top of the hill onto Main Street and drive as far as you can go. You might even see their cars there. But if you climb on top of the rocks, you can look down on the east side where they were camped and get the drop on them if they are there at the camp."

Both men ran for their cars and took off. We just stood there in the doorway feeling very let down that the men escaped, and it was partly our fault for putting the lead bars in the box. If we'd just taken the gold and left the box empty, they wouldn't have had the tools to escape with.

And there was another problem.

"Do you think they'll come back looking for the gold after they discover they have lead bars? You know they'll suspect us," Dean worried.

That worried me, too. They definitely knew who Dean was now, and they'd seen all of us enough to recognize us. There weren't many kids our age in the area and we weren't hard to find. We needed to have a long discussion with the Treasury Agent and Deputy Kingsman. It was looking like we needed to move to Australia!

Dean and I nailed the boards back in place on the floor and shoveled the gravel back on it to hide it to keep Mr. Simpson from getting suspicious that someone had been in the garage, then we left to go back to Dean's place and wait for the officers.

Mason and Kingsman drove up the hill and parked at the end of the road. There were no other cars there but there was a chance they had climbed the other side of the hill and were meeting at the campsite, so they crept cautiously up the backside to the top. They peered over the edge and could see a tent and other camping gear, but no sign of life. They would have to go down to the campsite and check it out.

They worked their way around the top side of the rock until they found a path down and then moved slowly toward the campsite. There was no one around and judging by the cold campfire, no one had been there for several hours. It was a dead end. They walked back to the cars and discussed some plans to locate the three men but without any real luck figuring out where to search next. It would be a good idea to put out an APB (all points bulletin) and patrol the area for about 4 miles around and watch for any one moving across any of the fields. If they were in their cars, they were already too far away to catch up to but maybe a roadblock would catch them farther away.

They drove back down the hill and split up, each taking a different road and traveling in every direction out about 4 miles, returning, taking another road, and repeated the procedure as many times as necessary.

About an hour later they gave up the search and came back to Dean's place. All of us were in Dean's office.

"Did you have any luck finding them?" Arlen asked. Arlen had remained in the office after getting the morse code transmission from me in case he was needed to make any more telephone calls.

"No, I'm sorry to say we didn't," Mason admitted. "We searched a radius of about 4 miles in every direction that we could drive, but they either have a good hiding place or they are in their cars far from here by now."

"What do you think they'll do now?" Dean asked nervously. "They know what we all look like, and they are bound to suspect that we took the gold. Do you think they'll come looking for us?"

"Probably not," Mason said. "What would be the point? If you took the gold, as they might suspect, they would also suspect that you turned it over to us. They would have seen the sheriff's car in front of the house when they left the garage, so they know the police are involved. They probably don't know the Treasury Department is on their trail yet, but they'll definitely know the sheriff's office is. My guess is they'll lay low until nightfall, then make their way a long ways from here and disappear again. Our only hope would be to find where they stashed their cars while waiting for nightfall if they haven't already left in the cars. But the two of us can't do it, so I'm calling in the State Police and more county officers. We need to comb this entire area on foot for at least five miles from Woodstock, maybe more if they kept going. However, five miles in an hour would be a pretty fast hike without trying to stay concealed while you did it. I think they are closer."

Mason asked to use the phone and he made a few phone calls. Within half an hour Woodstock was full of squad cars and the men from the Sheriff's posse with horses. There must have been at least 50 men ready to scour the area. Fifteen minutes later they had plotted out everyone's route and they were all ready to head out.

Mason thanked us for our help and told us that they had everything under control now.

"Well, boys, you did a great job," Mason said. "You didn't know I was tailing you? I've had my eye on Thompson since he left prison, thinking he might lead us to the two missing bars of gold, but you guys kinda got caught in the middle."

"We saw you tailing us," I said. "At least we suspected we were being tailed, but we thought it might be more thieves looking for a share of the gold. What are you going to do with the gold now?"

"I'm going to take it to the bank in Richland Center for safe-keeping as soon as we complete our search. You can be sure they will be in a place where Thompson or Sweeny will never be able to recover them. Well, I'd better get going. Here's my card. If you get any more clues, you be sure to give me a call."

I assured him we would. He left with all the other men to start their search.

Ma had seen all the commotion and I could see her coming down the road to Dean's office with Grandpa in tow.

"What is all the commotion in town?" She asked.

I told her everything. Grandpa was standing there with a big grin on his face. Ma was fit to be tied.

"That is one of the best cases you boys have ever been on, even if it is only your second case," Grandpa said.

"Dad, stop encouraging them," Ma yelled at Grandpa.

"I'm not encouraging them," he said. "I was just admiring what a great job they did. Why, there isn't a detective agency in the whole state of Wisconsin that could have done a better job of locating that stolen gold," he said. "I think they have done an admirable job that most grown men couldn't do."

"Well, that may be true," Ma had to admit. "But that doesn't excuse the fact that they never told us what kind of danger they were getting into."

I spoke up, "We just got into it a little bit at a time. It never looked dangerous. We were just observing at first. It only got out of hand right at the very end and we certainly didn't see it coming, but fortunately we had planned ahead and were able to overcome all the problems. Now that took some pretty careful thinking on our part, so I don't see that we did anything wrong. We just had to do what we believed was right. And besides, this time we didn't even land in jail!"

"Staying out of jail and knowing right from wrong. That's a very adult step in life," Grandpa laughed as he defended us. "I think you boys should be given a medal for your ingenuity. Just look at how much good came of all this. They recovered over $30,000 in stolen gold. I think there should at least be a finder's fee."

Ma still wasn't convinced that we were such heroes. But she'd eventually come around. Just about that time Dad and Dean's dad both came home almost simultaneously. Dad saw Ma waving at him and yelling as he stepped out of the car so he came over to Dean's place. We went over the whole story with them one more time.

Our dads were much more proud of the outcome than our mothers were. But it would all smooth out over time.

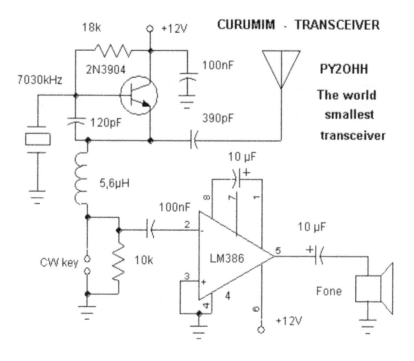

CURUMIM - TRANSCEIVER

PY2OHH

The world smallest transceiver

10

Later that evening the search parties returned. They hadn't turned up any clues. I started suspecting the criminals were closer than they anticipated, but I still couldn't figure out where they had hidden their cars. It was getting late and the search parties headed back to town for some supper as did Arlen. He was so proud of his new pocket radio because it had worked very well and came in real handy in this crisis. Dean was now chomping at the bit to get his ham radio license so he could have one of those pocket radios, too, after he heard how I called for help on my radio.

I could wait no longer. "Here, Dean, I made one for you too. Of course you can only listen to Arlen and me when we use ours as you won't be able to transmit until you get your Novice license, but I thought you might enjoy one for now."

I've never seen Dean so surprised.

"Wow, thank you. I didn't know you were building more than two of them. This is a great present. I've really got to work harder on my morse code now."

"I thought that might help pique your interest a little more," I said.

Dean went up to the house for supper and Grandpa and Grandma came over to our house to have supper with us and discuss the case some more. Dad and Grandpa were so busy trying to come up with some clues about where the criminals could have escaped to that Ma didn't have a chance to do any scolding, and by tomorrow she'll have calmed down a lot.

I went to bed early, really tired. It had been a long, hard day and we had missed dinner, so I was really out of energy.

But I had a hard time getting to sleep. I tossed and turned and when I did fall asleep, I had nightmares of things going much worse than they did.

In the morning I woke up exhausted and was still only half

awake, but I got out of bed, washed my face, and had some hot oatmeal for breakfast with bananas in it. I was still trying to think of what happened to those crooks. There was an explanation in there somewhere, but I hadn't come up with it yet, and maybe never would, but I just couldn't quit thinking about it.

What would I have done if I were those guys? Find a place to hide. But where? Where was a safe place to hide? An empty house? There weren't many in town, only a couple that I could think of. In the movies, the bad guys always broke into a house with people living in it and used them as hostages. That made the most sense, but whose house could they be in that was close to the scene of the crime? My imagination was running wild with the possibilities.

So I developed a plan. I would go to all the neighbors' houses and ask them if they had any jobs for me. A young boy always needs some spending money! Then I could get a feel for the situation and see if any of them were acting nervous like a hostage would. It was worth a try.

First I went to the store to ask John a question.

"Hi John," I said as I walked in the door.

"You're out shopping early today," John replied.

"All I'm shopping for is information. Did you see the commotion here yesterday?"

"Yes, Mr. Brewster told me later what it was all about. I guess you guys almost caught some thieves, but they got away, he said."

We had agreed, at Dean's last night, that none of us would mention the gold, nor the fact that it was now in the custody of the Treasury Department just because the fewer people that knew the whole story, the safer we'd be.

"Yes, it was a bad break. Have you had any strangers come in and get a lot of groceries lately?" I asked.

"Not really. There was some feller a few days ago that bought gas and some groceries. I asked him if he was from around here and he said he was just passing through. Nothing suspicious about that," John said.

"That's true. I was just asking for our investigation. We are still trying to find the guys that escaped. I thought maybe they didn't go too far and might be holed-up nearby and would need food."

"Are you helping that Treasury man find them?" He asked with a grin. I told him we always try to help the law, and didn't give any more information. It was time to go looking for a job. However a stranger getting groceries a few days ago could add up to the thieves planning ahead and stocking groceries some place to hole-up close by.

I grabbed my bike and went around the block and across the street from the garage to Harry Simpson's place to see if he and Bessie were OK.

I arrived at Mr. Simpson's place and I knocked on their door.

"Hello, there, Slim. How are you today?"

"I'm fine Mr. Simpson. I was wondering if you had any odd jobs around the place for me?"

"Well, I don't hardly think so, but we appreciate you asking. I've got the leaves all raked up, but maybe some other time."

"Ok, thanks," I said.

Well, he certainly wasn't acting nervous, so it appeared the men weren't there. However, to be sure I did peek in Mr. Simpson's garage to see if there were any vehicles in it that weren't his, but just one of his was sitting in the driveway and the other one was in the garage. Time to go to Chet and Erma Braun's place.

I went to Braun's, Neefe's, Braithwaite's, William's, Mrs. Coy's, and upstairs to Earl Sugden's, down Wolf Lane to Ray MacDaniel's, up to Dewey Brown's, and I looked in everyone's garage, then I started up Southshore Drive. The first house on the corner was Ova and Emma Burns' place. Ova had a huge garage/workshop and I hadn't seen anyone around for a while. I thought they might be visiting Ova's sister in RedGranite, Wisconsin because they went there quite a bit. I pulled in the driveway, parked my bike and walked to the garage. All the windows had curtains over them so I couldn't see in, and the door was locked. I went up to the house and knocked on the door, but no one answered. I checked his mailbox and it had several days of mail in it. So they were gone, apparently. I made a mental note to keep an eye on the place.

Then I got my bike and rode up the hill to check on Mrs. Armstrong, and I checked on Drayson's place, but they have a lot of kids, so I knew no bad guys were staying there. There were no cars at the top of the hill, so they hadn't returned to the rock. Then I rode half a mile farther up Southshore drive to the very end at Wooly's place. They were farmers and they were out working in the field. That meant no bad guys keeping them hostage. On my way home I rode up the little hill next to the road to look in the old hay barn that belonged to Drayson's, but they hadn't used it in in years. It was full of old, loose hay, from back before they started baling hay. It was a popular hangout for some of the older kids that lived out of town to bring their girlfriends for some necking.

Nothing looked unusual in the hay barn. But it did seem unusually full of hay. More than the last time I had looked in the barn. I found an old pitchfork in the corner and started poking the hay and moving some of the big stacks around and then my pitchfork hit something hard. I carefully started moving hay away from the object. It was a car, it appeared. I kept moving hay away until I could see a fender. It was a dark colored Studebaker. Our first clue. I quickly piled the hay back over it again, then I had a better idea. I went around to where the front of it would be and moved hay out of the way until I could see the hood. I unlatched the hood and then removed the coil wire so it couldn't be started, then I closed the hood and covered it back up with hay. I stuck the coil wire in my pocket.

Somewhere there was a 1957 black and white Rambler hidden, but it wasn't in the hay barn. We had to locate that car next. I double checked the barn that I hadn't left anything out of place, put the pitchfork back where I found it and got on my bike and left towards home.

All the way home I kept mulling over the clues in my mind. There were no places I hadn't checked in Woodstock for them to be hiding except the old Tyler place on the hill, and we had permission from Mr. Tyler to go in that any time we wanted, so I headed for that house.

I rode up the driveway and parked the bike then I went to the garage. It was still empty like we had left it during our first case earlier this summer. I had pulled back the curtains in the house the last time we were there so I could walk around the house and look in the windows without needing a key to get in. I looked in all the windows and there was no sign of any activity. It was still sitting empty and the door was still locked. Well, that left only one place that I couldn't account for and that was Ova Burns' place. It was time to get some help.

I stopped at Dean's on my way home.

"Hiya Mr. Brewster," I hollered as I walked into the shop.

"Well, Andy Rooney, I do declare," he ribbed me. "Catch any new criminals today?"

"No, no new ones, but we're still working on the old ones." He had a hearty laugh.

"I'm not interested in the criminals," he said. "I want to get my hands on the gold bullion."

"You wouldn't be able to keep it anyway. It's stolen."

"I know, but I just want to see what it feels like! Charlie Chan is in the office."

I walked into the office and Dean was sitting at his desk studying something.

"Whatcha studying today?" I asked.

"I'm studying the Novice ham radio test. I'm going to get my license pretty soon. You and Arlen are having too much fun."

"Well, the written test is pretty easy," I said. "It's learning the code that takes a lot of time."

"I know, I know," he said. "Just give me some time and I'll get it memorized. What you doing out and about today? You been fishing?"

"No, I need your help."

"I'll bet you do. You need some company in jail, probably," he predicted.

"Well, just for that remark I might change my mind about lending you my Knight Kit Star Roamer 5-band radio that I built last year. You could listen to ARRL's W1AW morse code training programs to help you with your code."

"I'm sorry. I'd really like to borrow your radio. Dad said he'd buy me a nice transceiver if I get my license. What do you need help with?"

"I don't think those crooks ever left town," I said.

"What makes you think so?"

I pulled out the coil wire from my pocket and threw it down on the desk in front of him.

"What's that from?"

"It's from Sweeny's Studebaker," I said.

"Where in heck did you get that?" Dean about burst.

"I took it out of his car."

"Where did you find his car?"

"It's hidden under hay in Drayson's old hay barn. I found it while I was looking for the crooks this morning. I thought maybe they were still in town and holding one of the neighbors as hostage while they hid out, so I asked everyone in Woodstock if they had any jobs for me, a young boy always needs money. Nobody did, but it was obvious they weren't nervous so I didn't think they were being held hostage, and I looked in everyone's garage to see if I could find the cars. I couldn't, so when I was coming back from Wooly's place I stopped in the old hay barn and it looked like there was more hay in it than before, so I took a pitchfork and started checking under the hay piles and I found the Studebaker. With hay being piled up on the car, it made it look like there was a larger stack of hay now. So I removed the coil wire and covered it back up. But the problem was, I still hadn't found where they were hiding out. There were only two logical places left, the old Tyler house and Ova Burns' place. I checked the Tyler house and there was nothing there. I checked Ova's place and the garage is locked up tight with curtains over the windows so I couldn't see inside. Nobody is home at Ova's and the mail has piled up so I figured they were visiting his sister in RedGranite. So there's a good possibility that the crooks are hiding either in the house or the garage and we need to start a surveillance on Ova's place until we determine if they are there."

"We might be able to keep an eye on it ourselves," Dean said. "If it gets to be too much work we could get Arlen or Danny to come help us part time."

"That's what I was thinking, too. It'll be easy to watch because we can see it from our fishing hole and we can see it from my house and your office, except your office doesn't have a window on that wall, so you'll have to go outside."

"Wrong, it does have a window. It's just covered up with wallboard to make more wall space for shelves when this used to be a store. We can open it up by taking that one panel off the wall."

So we got a couple screwdrivers and removed the sheet of wallboard and there was the window. It just needed a good cleaning, but it was in a perfect spot to watch Burns' place.

Upstairs at my place was a little more challenging. The only window I could watch from was in the storage room. Not as handy as watching from my room, but it was workable. We decided we'd go fishing, where we could watch the place.

11

We gathered up our cane poles and headed over to our fishing hole. We could sit on the bank in the shade, listen to the sound of the creek sneaking past us, hear an occasional minnow jump in the water, and absorb the beautiful songs of the meadow larks. It was September and the leaves were nearly all off the trees except along the creek banks where they had plenty of water. All was quiet over at Ova's place but we kept a good watch trying to figure out if anyone was staying in the house, or in the garage. It was still a wild guess at this point. There was no evidence they were even in town, but nobody found any evidence that they had left town either, and I had just about exhausted my theory that they never left town. There just wasn't anywhere else they could be. If I was wrong, we were going to waste a lot of time watching an empty house, but we'd get in a lot of fishing.

The morning passed quickly and soon it was dinner time. We hadn't had a bite all morning and we were wondering what change there was going to be in the weather that put the fish off their feed today. Watching the house continuously was not high priority as we only had to catch sight of some movement either in the garage or the house. Time was on our side during the day. It was at night that worried me. We couldn't watch the place all night, every night, but I sort of figured that if we could watch all of one night, someone would make a mistake and show a light. They were bound to get antsy and start moving around, maybe even try to take a walk at night when they felt it was safe. A man can only sit around just so long. Pretty soon they'd need some exercise and make a move.

We each went home for dinner. When I walked in the house Ma was busy with the ironing.

"Catch any fish today?" She asked.

"Not even a nibble all morning," I said. "There must be a

storm coming. I guess we'll just go bike riding after dinner for something to do."

"You could go swimming," she said.

I really wanted to go swimming but we couldn't see enough of the house and garage from the swimming hole. We needed to be in sight of them all day. Fishing, playing catch in Grandpa's yard, bike riding around the block, and watching from Dean's office or our upstairs window were just about our only options, but there wasn't much else we could do for a few days.

After a dinner of a peanut butter, jelly and banana sandwich, milk and cookies I went back over to Dean's. We got our bikes and started riding around the block and up and down Southshore drive, continuously glancing at the garage and house. We stopped alongside the grader ditch across from Ova's house and picked some wild blackberries growing along the road, talking and watching and just killing time.

After about an hour of that we got our ball gloves and went to Grandpa's big yard and started playing catch. Our heart wasn't in it and we missed catching the ball a lot because our attention was mostly on Ova's place. If anyone would have been watching us, it would have looked pretty obvious. But if they could see us, we could see them, too.

About 3 o'clock we walked over to the store and got a bottle of pop and a snack. John was watching TV when we walked in.

"You boys look hot and tired. What have you been doing?" John quizzed us.

"We were bike riding, then playing catch," I replied. It's pretty warm out there today."

"Yes it is. You can sit in here for a spell and watch some TV while you drink your pop," he offered.

"Thanks anyway," I replied, "but we'll sit outside on your bench where there's a cool breeze."

We paid for the pop and popsicles and went outside where we could watch the house and garage.

"Do you really think they are hiding at Ova's place?" Dean asked.

"Like I told you, I've used up all my ideas. If they aren't there, then they really did manage to escape town without getting caught, but that seems pretty unlikely and it certainly wouldn't explain what happened to their cars. And since I found one of the cars, the other has to close by. That's my opinion and I might be wrong, but it's the only lead we have to go on right now, and we don't have much else to do, so we'll give it a few days of watching. Maybe Ova and Emma will return home and end the mystery, but for now, there's still hope that we have found them and can trap them."

"Ok," Dean said. "I'll go along with that line of reasoning. It's our only hope to close this case. I sure hate to leave a case only half closed. It's great we could return the stolen gold, but I sure feel like we are only half done."

This was coming from a guy that never wanted to get involved in the first place, but he's hooked now!

We sat there in the warm fall sun and sucked on our popsicles and drank our pop. After about half an hour we decided we'd better move along so as not to attract any attention.

We decided to walk up the creek behind Ova's garage and look for another fishing hole, but be able to watch the garage and the house from the rear. We walked over to the bridge and dropped down under it. From here we had a good view of the rear of the garage and side of the house. We sat under the bridge for a while just watching the place, then we started walking slowly up the creek until we were almost out of sight of the house, then turned around and came back down under the bridge.

"This is getting real boring," Dean concluded. I had to agree. We weren't getting anywhere. If they were in there, they wouldn't be very likely to be seen during the daytime. We concluded that we'd take turns tonight watching the place, which meant we should take some naps during this afternoon so we could stay awake tonight. If we had one more person, we could stake out the place in shorter shifts during the night so I decided to go to Dean's and call Arlen.

"Hi Mrs. Bailey, is Arlen near the phone?" I asked.

"Oh, hello Slim. I think I saw him out in the shed. Let me go get him."

Pretty soon Arlen came to the phone.

"Hey, I can't say too much here but do you think you could come spend a couple nights here at my place? I'll explain later."

"Hang on. Let me ask."

Pretty soon he came back to the phone.

"Yep, everything's all set. Want me to bring a sleeping bag?"

"Yeah that would be OK, but we've got everything else we need, just bring your pocket radio," I said. "You can come down about supper time and eat with us. I'll let Ma know you are coming."

"Ok, see ya soon," Arlen replied. He knew something big was up when I told him to bring his radio.

We walked over to my place and I told Ma that Arlen was coming down to spend a night or two goofing off with Dean and me. Ma was always open to having one of the boys come spend the night so it was no problem and she especially liked Arlen and felt a little sorry for him because he had no brothers at home to do anything with, and he didn't have any close neighbor boys either without coming down here to join to us.

"Will he be here in time for supper?" Ma asked.

"Yep, I think he'll be here by about 4pm," I said. "There isn't any water near him for fishing and he just never gets to do much in the summer, so we thought he'd like to do a little fishing before school starts."

"Well, I'm sure he'll have a good time with his two best friends. Just stay out of trouble," Ma said.

"Of course, Ma. We don't have any trouble planned at all for a couple days," I replied.

"You know what I mean, and don't get sassy," Ma scolded.

"OK, I promise you we'll try to stay out of jail," and Dean and I laughed. "We are going back to Dean's to get some fishing gear ready. If Arlen stops here first, just send him over." Ma agreed.

I went upstairs and got my Knight Kit shortwave radio and we took it over to Dean's office.

"Let's string a long wire antenna for you out the side window,"

I said.

So we got the tools we needed and a spool of copper wire from his dad's bench, set the radio on his desk and ran a wire from it up to the ceiling and over to the wall by the window. If we could drill a hole in the wall by the window we could run a short piece of insulated wire through the hole and not have to have the window open to run the wire outside, so we asked his dad for permission.

"Dad, would it be OK to drill a tiny hole in the wall next to the west window in the office so we can run an antenna wire out it?" Dean asked.

"Sure, I'll help you," his dad said. "Now you know that if the wire touches the sides of the hole it will be grounded and you won't get any signal. So let's run an insulated wire from the radio and out through the hole, then attach the bare copper wire on the outside of the house to run to the trees for your antenna."

He got the drill and a bit and some insulated wire, then went to the office and went to work. In about 10 minutes we had everything in place and the hole sealed around the insulated wire to keep out water, and the wire reached about 100 feet along the creek and at a 45 degree angle to top of a small poplar tree. That would work perfect. We thanked his dad and then went back to the office to try the radio. Everything worked fine and now he'd be able to listen to the W1AW radio station and practice his morse code.

"Your dad sure was a big help," I said.

"He is always interested in helping me with my hobbies," Dean replied. "I told him I wanted to get my ham license and he thought that was a great idea and he encouraged me and that's when he said he'd buy me a nice radio transceiver if I get my license."

About half an hour later Arlen arrived.

"What's up guys?" Arlen asked.

"Oh, nothing," I replied. "Just trying to put a finish to our gold bullion case."

"How are you going to do that after the bad guys got away?"

"We don't know that they did get away," I said.

"You mean they might have caught them?" Arlen asked.

"Not yet, but maybe soon with our help," I replied. Then I told Arlen the whole story about my suspicion that they never left town and how we had narrowed it down to Ova Burns' garage or house. And I told him our idea to keep watch on the house all night and that's why we needed more help.

"If we're that close to catching them, I certainly want to be in on the final chase," he said.

Just then a sheriff's car drove past the store heading toward Ova's place. We stepped outside to watch it. He got to the intersection, stopped and looked around, then slowly drove up the hill and turned around on Main Street. He came back down the hill and stopped at the intersection again, looking around, then turned left and headed back down Woodstock drive toward Kingsman's place.

"I knew they had an APB, All Points Bulletin, out for those guys and the roads were being monitored all over the county, but it looks like Kingsman has some ideas of his own," I said.

"Let's hope he doesn't suspect Burns' place. We need to beat him to the punch," Arlen commented.

"Maybe we should just tell him what we suspect and let them search the place," Dean suggested. "It would be a lot safer and save a lot of time."

"Safer, yes, but we started this case and we are going to crack it. We've done all the hard work locating those guys the first time, and finding the stolen gold. It's only right that we get the credit for closing this case. Besides, we aren't doing anything dangerous so don't get nervous now," I reprimanded Dean.

We got on our bikes and took Arlen on a ride past Ova's place and discussed our plans. Then we went down under the bridge and watched the place for a bit and made note of the possible exits. There wasn't much left to do so we headed home for supper. I invited Dean to join us so we could plan our campout upstairs where we could keep an eye on the house at night.

Dad was home from work and Ma was just putting supper on the table. It was still about an hour before sundown and the night hawks were starting their evening flight looking for bugs to snatch out of the air. They hunted just like bats except they didn't have echo-location, so they had to hunt while it was still light, or else by the light of a yard light.

Ma had cooked up a nice meatloaf with mashed potatoes and gravy and a lettuce salad on the side. I really liked the French dressing on my salad and in fact, it's the only thing I liked about a salad. For desert we had tapioca pudding.

After supper we went outside to the yard and played catch for a while until the fireflies started coming out. Now that it was getting dark we watched the house and garage a lot closer for signs of life. If they were going to stir, though, it would probably be in the middle of the night when everyone was asleep.

12

We sat at the table and played dominos with Ma and Dad and my sister until after 9 o'clock. Then Dean got permission to spend the night and we went upstairs to get ready for our night vigilance. We didn't put on pajamas, but stayed in our day clothes in case we had to go outside for any reason. We brought my work table into the storage room and turned off the lights and sat in chairs at the table discussing the possibilities of what could happen and how we could handle it. It's all about making plans. You should always have a plan, and a backup plan. Arlen and Dean laid their sleeping bags on the floor and went to sleep while I watched the house and garage. The luminous dials on my Timex watch showed it was 10 PM when they laid down and I was sitting there alone, keeping a lookout. There was nothing I could do in the dark except just sit there and watch.

At midnight I woke Arlen and we traded places. We were going to take two-hour shifts. I went downstairs and brought up a pitcher of water and some glasses before turning in.

At 2 AM, Arlen woke Dean to change shifts, and that's when things started to happen. As Dean woke up and looked out the window, he let out a surprised gasp and it woke me up, too.

"What's up?" I asked. "Did you see something."

"I was just getting up," Dean said, "and I glanced out the window and I could swear I saw a small light in the garage."

We were all wide awake now and staring out the window. There it was again. Just a very quick flash. Could it have been a light from something reflecting on the glass windows from outside, like maybe a falling star or a plane flying over? Or was it coming from inside? We couldn't tell for sure.

Pretty soon we saw a figure of a man in the moonlight at the corner of the garage. He was standing there, looking around. Satisfied that he was alone, he motioned over his shoulder to someone behind him. Two more men joined him in the dark. The moon was at a waxing crescent and there was just enough light to see them, but not clearly. They walked very slowly into the driveway of the garage and stopped to look around some more. Then they proceeded to Southshore Drive and started walking east toward the store. We watched them cross the road and walk in the grader ditch. It was more concealed and much more quiet walking. They crossed our driveway, down our grader ditch, crossed the creek and then climbed up on the road and walked across to Dean's dad's shop.

"I know what they are up to," I said. "They are going to break in the shop and look for the gold bars where they suspicion Dean must have hid them. They think we have the bars and are keeping them from the law."

Then a wild plan jumped into my head.

"Shouldn't we call the police?" Dean asked.

"No, not yet. I've got a better idea," I said. "Arlen, you stay here with your pocket radio turned on and the earphone in your ear. Dean and I will go over to the garage. I want to sabotage their car."

"Are you crazy?" Asked Dean. "We should call the cops and they can catch them breaking into our shop."

"And if the cops don't get here in time, or they hear them coming, they might get to the garage and take off in their car. We need to strand them here so they'll be easier to catch," I said.

"Ok, then, let's get going, but under protest," Dean said. "We don't have much time."

We went downstairs and sneaked out the back door, around the house, across Grandpa's yard, and kitty corner across the road to Ova's garage. I had my earphone in my ear and my pocket radio turned on. We walked around the side of the garage to the side door. They had locked the door on their way out.

"Great, what do we do now?" Dean whispered.

"Let's check the windows. Maybe one is open," I said.

We walked alongside the building and checked each of the four windows. The third one was not only unlocked, but they had left it open a little for ventilation. I lifted the window and it slid up.

95

"Get down on your knees," I said to Dean. "I need a step-up to get in the window."

Dean got down on all fours and I stood on his back to reach the window so I could crawl inside which ended on top of a work bench. Once inside I took out my penlight and made my way to the black and white Rambler sitting in the middle of the garage floor. I located the hood latch, raised the hood, located the distributer, pulled the coil wire out of it and put it in my pocket. Then I carefully closed and latched the hood and went back to the window. I climbed back up on the work bench and out through the window onto Dean's back, then we lowered the window to the same amount it was when we found it.

"Did you get the coil wire?" Dean asked.

"Yep, and I put everything back the way it was. They won't even know we were here."

Just then I heard Arlen on the radio.

"S-C-R-A-M" the radio said, (di di dit, da di da dit, di dah dit, di dah, da da). Someone or all of them were coming back. We dropped behind the garage and down the bank, then east to the bridge where we could hide under it.

"They didn't stay at your place very long," I said.

We poked our heads above the edge of the road and watched. There was just one guy coming down the grader ditch.

"OK," I said, "It looks like just one of them is coming back. Something must have gone wrong. Maybe they can't get in."

"Dad put double deadbolt locks in each door," Dean said. "Maybe it's giving them trouble just getting in."

Pretty soon the man came back out of the garage and was going back toward Dean's. As soon as he disappeared we went alongside the garage, crossed the road, dropped into the grader ditch and headed back home. I telegraphed Arlen to keep watch and that we were going to go closer to Dean's place.

We cut back across our yard and around the back of the house, then we crossed the creek and cut across John Walters' back yard, around the back of the store and out to the road by the gas pump where we could see the front of Dean's garage. It looked like the man had brought back a small hammer and a crowbar. They were planning on doing some damage and we didn't want that to go any further.

"I've got an idea," I told Dean. "You stay here in the shadows. I'm going to go over by the old Tyler house, then I'm going to give a whistle. You answer with a whistle, but stay hidden. We want to scare them away, make them think they are being watched. If they don't run away, I'll holler at you from the shadows and you holler back. We'll make enough commotion that we will either scare them away or wake up the neighborhood."

So I quickly ran around the back of John's rental house on the corner, across the street and under one of the big trees on Tyler's hill, and then I let out a screaming loud whistle. Dean replied with a like whistle. The men at the door froze. They crouched down and looked around. I yelled, "Hey you. What are you doing?"

Dean yelled, "I see you."

The men dropped their tools and ran around the far side of the shop and disappeared into the shadows. I knew they were heading back to the garage but they might have to swim the creek to get there. I ran back to Dean and we headed across the road to the shop where Dean unlocked the door and we went inside. I immediately dialed the sheriff's department in Richland Center. We knew Deputy Kingsman would be on duty and not at his house. When they answered the phone I started telling them our story, but all of a sudden a large hand reached over my shoulder and took the phone from my hand.

13

"I'll take that phone," said the voice of a large man dressed all in black. It was Treasury Agent Mason. He took the phone and told the dispatcher exactly what he wanted, then hung up the phone.

"Well, you've done it again, boys," he said. "You've interfered with another investigation. I'll talk to you more about that in a little bit but for right now, I want you to promise me you'll stay right here, out of sight and out of hearing. Lights stay off. No noise." We promised, nervously, and he left.

"Oh boy, now you've really gotten us into trouble again. He was talking about jail time, I'm sure of that," Dean said. "I think we need to call your grandpa. We're going to need a good lawyer."

For once I agreed with him. I grabbed the phone and called Grandpa.

"Grandpa?" I asked

He answered, "Slim? What in tarnation are you doing calling at this time of the morning?"

"Grandpa, I think we're in trouble again." I gave him a very brief description of where we were and told him we'd need a good lawyer. He said he'd be right over and then hung up the phone.

Then I telegraphed Arlen and told him we might be under arrest. I said, "come if you want to, or stay out of it." He telegraphed back, "Ok, coming." He didn't want to miss any excitement. Arlen sneaked out the back door, down the creek, and across the road and into the office.

"What's up?" He asked.

I quickly told him everything that went on since the time we left the house and I pulled out the coil wire and threw it on the desk.

"They aren't going to get away this time," I said.

We looked out the side window watching Ova's garage. In the moonlight we saw three men cross the bridge, after having swum across the river, on their way to garage, then they disappeared around the edge of the garage. Pretty soon we saw a lone man, Agent Mason, cross the road heading toward the garage. The large garage doors swung open and we could hear the starter on the car grinding, then there was a gunshot and all of a sudden the whole town came alive with sirens and squad cars, all converging on the garage, spot lights aimed at the garage, men talking on their megaphones, hollering at the men inside to come out. Two police dogs were on leash being held back, snarling and growling and barking toward the garage, straining at their harness to be let loose to tear apart the convicts. The sheriff's deputies held them back. Everyone had their guns drawn. The lights in the garage all came on and I could hear someone shouting but we couldn't make out what was being said.

Pretty soon Agent Mason came out with three men in front of him at gunpoint. One man was holding his arm and I guessed that's what the gunshot was all about. Six deputies and two State Patrol officers converged on the men, handcuffed them and took them into custody.

Just then Grandpa came in the door. He said he'd been standing outside watching the excitement.

"What kind of trouble are you boys in, now?" He asked.

We told him everything that had happened this evening and that we thought Agent Mason was threatening to take us to jail as soon as he had time to deal with us.

"Well, I wouldn't be too concerned about that," Grandpa said. "You haven't done anything illegal, except maybe go in that open window to disable the car, that and maybe withholding evidence. However, you can't really call it evidence until you were sure they were in the garage, so I don't think that will stick in court," he said. Dean started to relax. Arlen and I weren't very afraid. After all, we'd all been in jail before, more than once, and it never amounted to anything. We had never really done anything wrong, but we certainly helped the law to nab some criminals, now on both cases. We were pretty sure we'd be heroes again after the law heard our side of the story. After all, it wouldn't look good for the officers if three or four kids solved all their cases for them!

We watched out the window and the officers were in the garage, probably looking for evidence to collect for court. The place was lit up like a circus. One officer was looking through Ova's mail, probably trying to tie them to hiding the crooks. The house was broken into by the State Patrol as they went inside to look for more evidence, but we were pretty certain the crooks had never been inside, but boy, was Ova and Emma going to be mad when they got home and had to fix the lock on the door. Pretty soon a tow-truck showed up and the officers pushed the Rambler out of the garage and hooked it to the tow-truck, then they turned out the lights and shut the garage doors. Everyone left except one sheriff's car. It came over to the office and out stepped Mason and Kingsman. As they walked in, and we turned the lights on, I could see they had grins on their faces. Everything was going to be OK.

"The Woodstock Irregulars strike again," Kingsman said.

I spoke up and said, "I can help you with that car." And I handed them the coil wire. "I took this out of their car so they couldn't escape you again," I said with grin.

They looked at each other and shook their heads.

"When did you steal this wire?" Mason asked.

"I didn't really steal it," I said. "I just borrowed it to show you. I was going to put it back, honest," I said with a grin. "When we saw the three men going over to Dean's place, Arlen kept watch from our upstairs and Dean and I went to the garage and borrowed the wire."

"It's a good thing you did," Mason said. "They got to the car before I got there and they would have given us a merry, and maybe deadly car chase to get them. This was a much neater way to nab them." Then they asked for the whole story, so we all sat down and recounted everything that happened from the last time we saw them.

"And, on top of that," I paused and grabbed the other coil wire off the shelf and handed it to Kingsman. "Here's the wire to their other car, the dark colored Studebaker. You'll find it buried in hay in Drayson's old hay barn at the turn in the road toward Wooly's farm." Then I had to tell them the story about how I'd found that car also.

"All's well that ends well," Grandpa said. "What's on the agenda for our next case?"

"Hold on there," Agent Mason said. "What makes you think there will be a *next* case? You boys have done a great job, it's too bad Danny isn't here to help put an amen to this caper, but you boys know very well that you are meddling in things that are very dangerous and only highly trained adults should be doing this kind of work. I'm not saying we don't appreciate all the work and fact-finding and clues you've solved to bring this case to a close, or the first case, which I've also been made very aware of, but just how many cases do you think can come to a small town like this? What you boys got involved in has to go down in the annals of history as being extremely rare incidences. I think you'll be able to lead normal lives now, fishing, riding bikes, mowing lawns, all the boring things young boys are supposed to be doing. You can do all this exciting work, and get paid for it, when you get older."

"And as your friend and neighbor, I want to tell you boys that when you turn 21, you are officially invited to apply to the sheriff's department for jobs helping us and I'll personally put in a recommendation for you," Deputy Kingsman added.

"And the Federal Government can use good agents in the FBI, the Treasury Department and the Secret Service if you are interested in going that route, also when you are 21," Agent Mason invited.

I spoke up and said, "That all sounds good, but that's a long ways off, and we still have a lot of cases to solve around here. Why, we are expecting a new case to break almost any day now! I wouldn't be surprised if I had to call on you guys again in the next few months."

Everyone laughed, but it wasn't as absurd as it sounded. As everyone was getting up to leave and go home, the neighborhood came alive. John and Hanzel from next door at the store, Ma and dad, Mr. And Mrs. Brewster, Theo Drayson and a few other neighbors were converging on the shop. Agent Mason and Deputy Kingsman said their goodbyes and we were trapped in the shop answering questions and retelling the story several more times. We were tired and wanted to go to bed. Finally Grandpa held up his hand to quiet everyone down and said, "Why don't we all go home now and let these heroes get some rest. You can read all about it in tomorrow's paper."

Everyone got up and left and Dean said he was going to sleep in his own bed the rest of the night. Grandpa, Ma, Dad, Arlen and

I walked across the road to our house. Ma was being unusually quiet.

Finally she said, "What did I tell you boys about staying out of trouble?"

"We were never in trouble," I defended. "We only helped catch some dangerous criminals, but the police did all the dangerous work. We just did everything the careful way. We didn't even go to jail this time!"

Ma was at a loss for words. She was beaten. We hadn't done anything wrong and we would probably be heroes in the paper again. She wouldn't admit it, but we knew she was actually proud of us. Dad and Grandpa weren't shy about it. They told everyone what heroes we were.

14

The next morning we got up much later than usual. Arlen and I slept in until almost 10 o'clock. We hadn't gotten much sleep the night before.

We sleepily stumbled down the stairs and Ma had hot oatmeal on the stove waiting for us. I was starved and had a big breakfast of oatmeal with bananas, toast, an egg and a glass of milk. Arlen outdid me and had two eggs. That really woke us up and got our day started. Just as we started to leave the house a sheriff's car drove by followed by a tow-truck. They were obviously going to retrieve the Studebaker from the hay barn. We stood and watched them go by and deputy Kingsman waved at us.

We walked over to Dean's place and Mr. Brewster was working in the shop. He shouted a hearty hello to us.

"It's the Hardy Boys on another case," He shouted as we walked in.

"The Hardy Boys were slackers," I replied. "We are much more professional. I've been thinking about hanging a sign by the front office that says, 'Woodstock Irregulars Investigations,'"

"You make up the sign, and I'll hang it up for you," he replied with a laugh. "Go on in, Sherlock is waiting at 221 B Baker street."

We walked into the office and Dean was at the shortwave radio trying to copy slow code.

"You've got to be faster than that," I chided him.

"I'm getting there. I'm able to pick out some of the letters already. Just give me some time. I should be ready by Christmas."

"Did you see the tow-truck go by?" I asked.

"Yep, with the deputy leading it. I guess they are going to pick up that Studebaker in the hay barn," he said.

"Yeah, that's what we we figure. Well, another case closed. What shall we do next?"

Arlen spoke up and said, "I was thinking that Danny and Dean and I should join the Lone Scouts and go to camp with you next summer."

"That's a crackerjack idea," I said. "This town could use a few more good scouts! It might even help on our next case."

"What *next case?*" Dean asked. "Haven't you guys learned your lesson yet? All we do is get into trouble with *your* cases."

"What trouble did we get into this time?" I asked. "Sure the officers warned us to not be doing their job for them, something about it being too dangerous or something like that, but who was listening to them? We made them look like boobs this summer solving all the local cases and nobody got hurt. Well, I take that back, Larry did get shot in the arm by Agent Mason, but Larry always was too quick with that gun!" And we all laughed. We looked out the window and Mr. Pauls, the mailman, was dropping off the mail in all the mailboxes.

"I'll bet even Mr. Pauls has heard about our latest adventure," I said.

"Yeah, well, I still say we were lucky not getting thrown in jail again," Dean spouted. "We did withhold information and we did steal the gold bullion, sort of, and kept it from the law until we were ready to present it. We really had lots of information we could have shared, like finding the Studebaker."

"Yes, but we couldn't just share our suspicions. Nobody would have believed us. I think I proved that in the last case when I told Ma the whole story and she thought I had too wild of an imagination. That's the way grown-ups are. They never believe kids. They think we just make up stuff. Anyway, it was a wonderful summer, full of adventure. I can't wait for next summer so we can find another case to work on."

Pretty soon Mr. Brewster came barging into the office with a newspaper in his hand.

"Look at this boys, you made the front page."

Sure enough there were the headlines of the Republican Observer, "The Woodstock Irregulars Recover Stolen Gold Bullion," and then it went on to describe our part in the big bust, which they must have gotten from one of the officers.

"It looks like we are famous again," I said.

"Now if they'd only pay for fame," Dean remarked.

"Maybe they have," Mr. Brewster said as he handed me an envelope. It was from the Bank of Milwaukee. I opened the envelope and there was a check for $3000 made out to me, Dean, Arlen and Danny. Turns out there was a 10% finder's fee. Wow, that would be $750 each. Now I wouldn't have to work on a farm all next summer to get money for that new 3-speed bike I'd been wanting.

"That sure came fast. How did they get that here so quickly?" Dean asked.

"I don't know for sure, but I'm guessing either they were notified we had found the bullion a few days ago, probably by Agent Mason, or else one of the officers put in a call last night to some emergency number of the bank and it came by special courier," I said.

"And they say crime doesn't pay," Arlen said. "It's paid us very well."

We all took the check over to show Grandpa and Ma and they were flabbergasted. Of course Ma had to spoil it.

"Well, young man, you know where that money is going to go, don't you?"

"Yes, it's going to buy me that new 3-speed bike I've been wanting for years."

"No, it's going into your college fund."

Grandpa intervened. "Rosy, I think putting $700 in the college fund is plenty. After all, you made him put all $250 of his reward money from the last case into his college fund. He earned that money with hard work and determination. He deserves a reward that he can enjoy now, not eight years from now."

Ma thought about it a little, then she agreed.

"Well, OK, you can have that much out of the funds for now, but the rest is for your education." We all agreed on it. Then I showed them the newspaper.

"Well would you look at that?" Grandpa said. He read it out loud very carefully. "That's quite a write-up. I'll bet you won't have any trouble getting dates now!"

"Getting dates?" We asked. "Who wants dates? We'd rather have clients contacting us to find lost treasures or missing persons, for a fee and expenses, of course," I said.

"Don't get your cart ahead of the horse," Ma replied. "You need to finish school before going into business."

Monday was Labor Day, and the last day of summer vacation. Tuesday through Thursday was going to be our first week of school. Friday was a teacher in-service day so our first week was going to be a short one, just enough to get us back into the habit of going back to work. That's what school always felt like. Up until you were six years old, every day of the year was an adventure, then you turn six and you had to go to first-grade and start working five days a week like an adult, except we didn't get paid for it. Life wasn't too bad while you still got summers off and a long two-week vacation at Christmas and a week at Easter, but it wouldn't be too long before we'd be working five or six days a week for 50 weeks out of the year when we got out of high school, or college, then life was pretty much over until you get old enough to retire. Growing up didn't really sound like any fun at all, but getting just a little older could help with our adventures. When we turned 16 we could get our driver's license and even a pilot's license, and when we turn 21 we could get a job in law enforcement, so that gave us something to look forward to. In the meantime, all we had was the Woodstock Irregulars and the next case we had yet to solve.

THE END

About the Author

Lon Lawrence, a 30-year native Wisconsin boy, grew up in a small town called Woodstock (pop. 50) which was 14 miles from the "city" of Richland Center (pop. 5000). He lived a block from Pine River where he fished and learned to swim, and squirrel hunted in the hills around Woodstock. He attended a one-room school house with all eight grades which was half a mile from town.

Mr. Lawrence graduated high school in Richland Center, Wisconsin and many years later graduated from the University of New Mexico, Albuquerque with a Major in Education and a Minor in Science.

As a private pilot he has published many magazine articles for various flying Magazines, was senior editor of Homebuilt Rotorcraft, and has published two previous books.

Having traveled by RVs all over the USA for 42 years, he now resides near Deming, NM with his wife, Mary, and 3 dogs. He is a Vietnam Veteran USAF, former teacher and police officer and enjoys motorcycling and shooting.

Made in the USA
Monee, IL
02 January 2025

72758891R00066